A BATTLE BETWEEN BLOOD

TALES OF AOLAS
A NOVELLA

J.D.L. ROSELL

This is a work of fiction. Names, characters, places, and incidents either are the product of the author's imagination or are used fictitiously. Any resemblance to actual persons, living or dead, events, or locales is entirely coincidental.

Copyright © 2024 by J.D.L. Rosell

All rights reserved.

Illustration © 2023 by René Aigner
Book design by J.D.L. Rosell
Map © 2023 by Keir Scott-Schreuder
Map colorization and chapter headers by Rachel St. Clair

ISBN 978-1-952868-46-7 (IngramSpark trade paperback)
ISBN 979-8-324014-57-5 (KDP trade paperback)
ISBN 978-1-952868-45-0 (ebook)

Published by Rune & Requiem Press
runeandrequiempress.com

AO|

- CRIMSON SEA
- YRALDI ISLES
- DHUULHEDI
- SENDESH CHYCHAXIL'ISK
- BURBAY
- THUNDER SEA
- THE FRINGES
- SISCES
- FELINAN
- AVOLICE
- CANTU
- DAREUX
- THE RUINS OF ERLODAN
- HUNT'S HOLLOW
- HALENHOL
- MISALAR
- AVENDOR
- EDENPOL
- GLADELYN
- HUSHED SEA

THE WESTREACH

- BEFA SPICE ISLES

THE FAR DEPTHS
OF DU'ORLAM

THE RAINWOODS

N

SHARVAL
THE RUINS OF
LETHYRANTH
DREYGOJ

VALE OF MISTS
NAFUAH
ASPAR
VALANKESH
PASS
IKVALDAR
VALANDUAI
RANGE
KYZAN
AGN
LOMHUI

JEDFOLD
HAUDDEN
KAVAUGH
TRADER
SPRINGS
LAKSIS
WASTES
REJEYA

FAERNOR
GRASSLANDS

BAVNY
KHWAM
WOODS
HILLS OF
DAVRED

LEISLE
SEA

KROBESH
SHIVAK NODH

THE
EMPIRE OF THE
RISING SUN

FOREWORD

Welcome back to Aolas, dear reader!

It's been two years since the original Legend of Tal series ended with *A God's Plea*. If you've read it—and it's best that you have if you intend to read this book—you know events wrapped up in a tidy bow.

…Or nearly so.

There's a rather significant gap between the last chapter and the epilogue in *A God's Plea*. A period during which our cast have many challenging and harrowing experiences. Most notable of these is the long, bloody civil war in Gladelyl, which largely takes place in its capital, Elendol.

This is where *A Battle Between Blood* picks up. I'll let the story give you the rest of the context, but as I said above, it's best enjoyed by those who have already read Legend of Tal.

If you need a reminder on the characters, creatures, or other aspects of Aolas, you will find appendices located near the end of the book.

One final note: You may also remember from the author's note in *A God's Plea* that this is not the end of the stories told in this world. In fact, this novella marks the beginning of the story universe I'm calling "Tales of Aolas."

FOREWORD

Tales of Aolas includes the Legend of Tal series and all the upcoming series set in this world. You wouldn't be far wrong to think of it as my version of the Marvel Universe or Brandon Sanderson's Cosmere.

But enough from me—it's past time you set into the story. May you enjoy the journey!

~ *Josiah (J.D.L. Rosell)*

Whoever fights monsters should see to it that in the process he does not become a monster himself. And when you look long into the abyss, the abyss also looks into you.

— FRIEDRICH NIETZSCHE, *BEYOND GOOD AND EVIL*

PROLOGUE

Every story begins with perspective.

This was a lesson that my mentor, Falcon Sunstring, often repeated before his passing. It is one I still find easy to ignore.

Perhaps it is because the events that follow exceed any one person. They encompass the entirety of our land. Not just Elendol where they occur, or even Gladelyl and the Westreach. They affect the whole of Aolas.

It is the tale of one war ending and the foretelling of the one still to come. We scarcely glimpsed what was fated. The blood waiting to be spilled. So do many tragedies unfold.

But there I go—already, perspective flees me. Let me begin anew.

This story tells of the end of my people's civil war. The final battle between those who shared blood. Neighbor pitted against neighbor. Kin against kin.

Father against son.

Then, we did not know Tal Harrenfel would return. Nigh on seven years had passed since we lost him and our other comrades to the false Whispering Gods. Yet with fighting filling the intervening seasons, we had scarcely healed. Scars lay open. Wounds wept daily.

While loss permeates our perspectives, that is not the heart of this story. That, I hope, I shall convey in due time.

Perhaps one day, I will capture this tale in song, as Falcon could have. For now, ink and parchment must suffice.

Come: Enter the grand forests of the Gladelysh elves. Walk among the roots of our lofty kintrees. Witness how we came to reclaim our home.

Even if we may still lose it.

—Rolan Venaliel, First Prince of Gladelyl, Royal Bard to the Court of the Elf Queen

1
NOOSE

"*Sen kord.*"

Garin breathed through the spell's transition. The clamor in his ears was like the gnashing teeth of a thousand ghouls, but it faded after a moment. His hearing settled and sharpened.

Words spoken hundreds of strides down the shadowed street became audible.

"Now, *kolfashi* cretin," a sneering voice said. An elven man's. "Submit or be made to!"

"Please, sir," a second begged, also male, voice accented with Imperial inflection. "I would bring you food—of course, I would—but our pantries... There's not enough for us to eat and none to spare. You would have us starve?"

Garin tightened his hand over his sword's hilt before forcing it loose again. Justice would come for them, inevitable as a dragon's descent. He would bring it.

Resolution did little to soften the blow. A squelch of flesh slapping against bark gauntlets rang in Garin's ears. The cry of pain cut deeper.

He couldn't loosen his grip on his sword now.

Say their name, he willed the unseen assailant. *Say it and seal your fate.*

"Let us try this again." The sadistic elf spoke more softly now. A veneer of reasonability. "I can be merciful, as can my mistress. But a queen must uphold order, do you not think?"

For Wren, the naming of "queen" would have been enough to condemn the elf. He was conscious of her at his back in the ill-lit alley, sword already drawn, her every noise brimming with impatience. She and the Ilthasi, the covert agents in service to the true queen, heard nothing of the exchange, awaiting Garin's confirmation to close in. He wondered if he had tarried too long already.

But he needed a name, *the* name. Justification for what would follow. Tyranny bred tyranny, and he wanted no part in a queendom that did not uphold the values it espoused, even in war. Especially then.

"O-of course," the Imperial stammered between sniffs. "I… I'll be back with what we have."

Garin swallowed a sigh and held up a hand to catch the others' attention. *Soon*, he mouthed.

His companions were difficult to see with his human eyes, but he trusted elven vision to be sharper. Once, Elendol had been illuminated day and night, werelights lifting the gloom cast by the impenetrable canopy above. But since war had fallen, the sorcerous lights had been extinguished, both sides seeking the cover of darkness to hide their movements. Only as the Crownless Queen took back each section of the city did she return the werelights to the sky.

In more than one way, Ashelia Venaliel was returning light to Elendol.

Garin soon heard the Imperial man return. The elves outside his home—more than one, he judged by their murmurs—shifted their feet, no doubt fanning out around their victim. Steel hummed as it left scabbards.

"This?" the male elf scoffed. There was the rustle of something being handled, then a squelch as it hit the ground. "Rotten! How *dare* you insult the Rightful Queen with this impudence? By the authority of Her Eminence, I will see that you suffer."

Garin's heartbeat almost drowned out the whimper that came next, and the blow that followed. *The Rightful Queen.* It was as good a sign of guilt as he would get. None called Ashelia that; to her Loyalists, she was ever the Crownless Queen.

Another claimed that title along with the crown and throne. Their adversary these long five years.

Maone Lathniel.

Once, the Peer of Elendol had merely been a nuisance, if a worrying one. She and those calling themselves Sympathists had undermined her predecessor, the now-deceased Geminia Elendola. All they had done had led to a fell sorcerer, the immortal Extinguished, summoning the devil Heyl and burning the capital a second time in three decades.

As Geminia lacked an heir, the throne fell to Maone. Since her crowning, she had only delved deeper into her sins. The city and all the elvish queendom of Gladelyl had suffered as Maone tightened her rule and squashed all who protested it. When the peoples she'd once pretended to support—the many bloodlines fleeing the tumultuous Empire of the Rising Sun to find refuge in Elendol—were persecuted, Ashelia, next in line for the throne, could no longer stand by.

Fresh from giving birth to her second son, still reeling from the loss of her beloved after he'd unseated Aolas's false gods, she rose to take what should never have belonged to House Lathniel. As her cause spread, many of the peoples, elven and otherwise, rallied to her banner.

Now, after five years, they were close to taking it all back. The noose had been tightening around those serving the false queen for these last months. Only this sector around the Lathniel kintree remained within her control.

At last, they would take it back.

He shook his head, easing out of the spell, and met Wren's eyes. The golden tendrils in them whirled faster, the brightest thing in the alley.

"Now!" he hissed.

None hesitated. As one, their party flowed from the alley and out onto the street. Though Garin went first, Wren quickly overtook him. The queen's agents, clad in dark clothes, were close behind, knives and rapiers bristling in their hands, every eye spinning with inherent magic.

Their quarry soon came into sight, a circle of illumination in the gloom. Shadows shifted as the figures moved. Fresh cries of pain told of the blows landing.

Garin pressed on as fast as he could. Their footsteps, kept soft through practice and enchanted shoes, would soon alert the enemy to their approach. He drew *Helshax*, the golden runes stark against the black steel.

The silhouettes parted, revealing steel glimmering above a crouched man—a medusal, the reptilian people hard to mistake. The final blow set to fall.

Garin stuttered to a stop, stretched out a hand, and shouted, *"Qed nenik und!"*

The clamorous Worldsong invaded his mind again, this time in a clatter of laughter and kitchenware, but he'd heard it too often to let it distract him. As the spell sapped his energy, he wove it around the distant man.

The sword came down—then halted.

Still at a distance, Garin could barely see what occurred. Where one medusal had been, now there were three, all in a similar huddle, and none where they'd knelt before. The elf looked between them and snarled loud enough for Garin to hear.

"Sorcery!"

His realization came too late. Wren and the Ilthasi had already reached the Royalists and begun cutting through them. The advantage of surprise was too much. In moments, the dozen men and women were cut down to half their number.

Garin sighed with relief before continuing his sprint. When he reached the melee, he found the medusal had crawled back to the safety of his home, a decrepit hovel nestled under one of the towering kintree's roots.

"Stay inside!" he told him, though the man looked to need no encouragement. Slitted pupils amid yellow eyes open wide, feathered ruff standing on end, the medusal slammed the door shut.

The Worldsong howled a warning.

Garin spun, sword leading, as the elf struck at him. Years of training kicked in. Adopting the Form of Water, he parried and slipped away, every movement fluid and his body loose.

The elf didn't give him time to get his bearings. With an assault combining force with form, he bore down on Garin, rapier whipping around in a storm too fast to follow. Skilled as Garin had become, the Dance of the Blade had never been his forte. Only the elven enchantments woven into his supple armor kept him from suffering fatal wounds.

But he had more than swords to bring to bear.

"Jolsh thasht!" A pummeling wind erupted from the hand Garin thrust toward the elf. Strong as a winter gale through a mountain pass, it barreled into his adversary and knocked him down.

The elf recovered quickly, falling into a roll that brought him back to his feet. He held his rapier before him, eyes spinning with malice.

Only then did Garin recognize who it was: the medusal's tormentor, the leader of the pack. His armor of enchanted bark, his bearing and disdain, and that he survived thus far pointed to his being trained in the Dance, as all Highkin elves were. Garin's education had been brief, his mastery of swordplay nowhere near the same level.

A glance around showed the others still occupied with the

last of the Lathniel roughs. Garin was on his own. But he'd faced down monsters and immortals, dragons and gods. A single elf, no matter how skilled, wasn't enough to rouse his fear.

The highborn elf charged again, blade leading, lips parting. Garin never heard the word that left his mouth, but its effect was apparent enough. Flames spread from the elf's free hand, blinding and blistering.

Garin held up *Helshax* against the spell. The dark sword drank in the sorcery like a lathered horse would water from a trough. As the elf hissed with surprise, Garin drove into the opening, hoping to gain a score of his own.

His efforts proved fruitless. After a flurry of blows, his black blade knocked against the elf's side, but the bark armor protected him. Garin took a shallow cut to his arm for his efforts.

Wincing, Garin adopted the Form of Stone and swept his heavier sword at the elf with both hands. The elf had no choice but to dodge, giving him a moment to breathe. It wasn't enough, though. Sorcery was his only path forward.

Freeing a hand, Garin called, "*Keld thasht!*" The Worldsong spiked in his ears, then heat left his body to burst in a plume of flames.

The elf cursed, spinning out of the way. He appeared to have evaded the worst of it, though his armor was scorched and the ends of his golden hair were singed.

Garin had only meant it as a distraction. Drawing in the Worldsong, he let its torrent fill him, numbing him to the violence of his intentions. Pointing his hand again at the man, Garin spoke with finality.

"*Thal ovth.*"

The elf, who had charged again, stuttered to a stop. His eyes widened, the bronze tendrils in them bright and spinning fast. His mouth fell open, but only a wordless scream issued forth.

He collapsed to the ground moments before blood burst through his skin.

Boil blood. Garin had long ago learned the translation of the words, but only after he'd spoken them against a bandit who had caught him in the woods. He hadn't known what would result from them.

His first kill.

Now, he felt only a sliver of guilt as he watched the man's lifeblood ooze from every orifice, painting over the light in his eyes. That was war. A grisly end for most.

Turning aside, he shivered away the chill from the casting and located his comrades. Two Ilthasi had been lost, but the last of the Lathniel men had finally fallen. The Crownless Queen's agents drifted back toward Garin as they scanned the shadows for more enemies.

Wren ran in the opposite direction.

"Wren!" Garin called, not sure if he was gladder to see her alive or exasperated that, once again, she was going her own way. "Dead gods, would you wait?"

"He's getting away!" was all she shouted as she turned down an alley heading around the Lathniel kintree.

Sighing, Garin jerked his head after her, then set off at a jog. The noose had some way more to tighten before it strangled their enemy. The night promised to be long.

It'll all be worth it, he thought, *if I can just keep that damned woman alive.*

2
WAR

*A*ir hissed through her teeth. Her body burned with exertion.

Wren didn't slow or pause. The fleeing Lathniel soldier turned a corner ahead, but she was closing on him. Heaving in another breath, she put on a fresh burst of speed.

The walkways of Low Elendol weren't meant for running. The Mire was what most called this part of the city, and for good reason. The ground was swampy and soft. The streets and giant roots of the looming kintrees were slick with moisture. Spray from the Sanguine River flowing through the city's center and droplets from the leaves of the towering canopy only worsened the situation.

But though she slipped with every step, she couldn't delay. Her quarry escaping could mean many more people dying, for the man would warn his false queen of the battles around the Lathniel kintree and drag out the conflict further.

This damned war had claimed far too many lives for her to let it take more.

Turning a corner, the ground opened up before her in a wide plaza that led to the base of the Lathniel kintree. Wood shaped by mages of the House formed a platform above the marshy ground. Between the fountains and gardens, both derelict after years of war, ran the escaping soldier, already halfway across the space. On the other side waited a lift to the upper heights of the kintree, where seven others stood guard.

Eight to one. Poor odds even for her. Wren never hesitated. With a clear view of her prey, she threw out a hand and shouted a word.

"*Wuld!*"

Her lungs flattened, the cantrip stealing the last of her breath. Yet as a gust blew from her hand to knock the man flat, she smiled savagely.

"Got you," she wheezed as she slowed to a jog.

The dazed elf was too slow to rise. Even as he shouted to those around the lift, she reached the escapee and drove down her sword.

Starbright blazed as it pierced his back, the enchanted blade biting deep into the soft wood beneath.

Placing a boot on the dying man, she withdrew her sword and faced the oncoming lift guards. Three raised bows with arrows nocked. The other four marched toward her, oaken shields and sharp sabers in hand. The tendrils in their eyes sparked beneath conical bark helms.

She took stock of her assets. Her sorcery left much to be desired, her quarter-elf blood conferring little aptitude for it and her impatience even less. At least with their hands occupied, they were unlikely to cast spells against her. She carried no shield beyond what she could conjure, and while her clothes were imbued with a measure of protection, they were made more for stealth than battle. Starbright hummed in her hand, the Origin-forged sword a gift from Ashelia that had served her well during the long civil war. The Crownless Queen had promised it would never break, and Wren had discovered other hidden qualities besides.

Yet a blade alone couldn't turn the tide. She had to rely on her training, honed in practice and war, as well as her wits. Those, at least, she'd never lacked.

Wren grinned at the oncoming guards and spread her arms. "I'm only one half-kin woman! You strapping lads can't be afraid of me."

As she'd hoped, their speed increased. The archers hurried to draw and aim their arrows. It wouldn't prevent them from missing, but haste could lead to mistakes.

She needed any opening she could get.

They timed their attack well. Three missiles whistled through the air as the line of elves reached her. Wren whipped her free arm around and shouted, "*Wuld veshk!*" A shield of air appeared to knock aside the flying shafts.

But it wouldn't turn back blades.

The four elves struck in conjunction. Wren adopted the Form of Air, her footwork quick and each touch of her sword light as she parried. Alone, it wouldn't have been enough, but a quick casting of a fire cantrip kept what swords she couldn't block at bay.

She retreated, seeking to funnel the enemies between the garden squares. Eager to reach her, they complied, two coming to pursue her. Yet as the other pair branched off to flank her, success promised to be fleeting.

Movement flickered in her peripheral vision. Wren raised her hand and cast an air cantrip in time to ward off three more arrows. Panting as the sorcery took its toll, she called upon her blade.

Starbright.

Energy pulsed through her. Her senses sharpened, her mind quickened. Her body felt supple and strong.

She grinned as the guards engaged her again.

"*Lisk!*" Instead of casting the cantrip at the men, she pointed at the wooden platform at their feet. Ice spread over the wood. The pair noticed a moment too late. Even elven grace couldn't save them from tumbling to the ground.

Wren only managed a single strike before she had to spin to engage a guard on her right. Snarling, she chopped at his shield and sword, hoping to break them. The most she was rewarded with were chips in each. Conscious of the others at her back, she sent the guard stumbling back with a kick to his shield, then faced the last of her assailants.

To her surprise, it was a woman, uncommon among elven warriors. Her lips were curled with disdain as she tested Wren's guard. Wren echoed her feeling as she parried and struck back.

"*Kald!*" she spat in her face, rewarded with a wince as the guard raised her shield against the flames erupting from Wren's hand.

But the pair who had slipped on the ice were behind their comrade, and the one she'd knocked back had recovered as well. This time, no gardens or fountains impeded their path. As all four closed in, another volley of arrows fell toward her.

She badly needed a win.

Keeping an eye on the arrows, Wren raised her hand at the last moment. "*Wuld bruin!*"

One arrow ricocheted away from the blast of air, but the other two turned and sped toward her quarries. The guards raised their shields against the arrows. Only one was quick enough. The other went spinning to the ground with a cry, an arrow lodged in his sword arm.

"Ouch," she commented as the other three advanced, the fourth tending to his wound. She didn't hold back a smile as the tendrils in their eyes spun faster, a sign of anger.

As one, they bore down on her.

It was all Wren could do to survive the trio of sabers. Parrying and dodging two, the third caught her leg, parting her pants across her thigh and biting into her flesh. Hissing, she blew the warrior back with a blast of fire, wishing their bark armor wasn't enchanted to not catch flame. The other two kept pressing forward. As she missed another dodge, a second cut appeared across her free arm.

Wren stumbled back, but none of them gave her room to breathe. She was slowing, making mistakes. As she engaged the soldiers again, she wracked her mind for a way to gain a moment's peace. All it would take was drawing more energy from Starbright, then she might end this battle on her own terms.

Delving back into her mind, she reached for the first viable spell and threw out her hand, her wound pulling with the movement.

"*Lorn ist!*"

The wooden floor at their feet split as thick, sinuous roots burst through. Guards were thrown to either side, one landing in a fountain. The other two, battered and baffled, were slow to rise.

Only then did Wren remember the archers.

Whirling toward the lift, she turned to see the arrows gliding toward her. She raised a hand, but she couldn't get out the word in time.

Before the arrows could land, wind buffeted the back of her head and rocked her forward.

Sweeping curly locks back from her face, Wren turned and found Garin and the four Ilthasi with him hurrying up the street. "Took you long enough," she quipped as she turned back to their enemies who had risen to their feet and were advancing with wary looks at the newcomers.

"Got lost," Garin puffed as he came up beside her and scanned the plaza. His black sword was bared and at his side, while his other hand was slightly raised, ready to cast fresh spells. "Looks like I arrived just in time."

"Don't go thinking you're some hero. I had it handled."

He snorted a laugh, but his amusement evaporated as the Lathniel warriors closed in again. The one who had landed in the fountain dripped and stumbled; the other two seemed to have recovered from their tumble. At a word from Garin, the Ilthasi sprinted past, heading for the archers and the lift.

Wren concentrated on her sword again before they reached them. *Starbright*, she supplicated it, and once more, it filled her with strength.

She met their strikes with a smile.

After years of fighting side by side—to make no mention of sharing a bed—the pair had learned to move as one. Wren met the two charging on the left while Garin took the one on the right. The injured warrior, she left to her beloved; the elf had sheathed his saber and raised a hand, clearly intent on sorcery.

Moving with renewed vigor, she parried with both cantrip and sword, then kicked the female guard's knee. She collapsed with a cry while Wren dodged her comrade's shield and hacked at his saber. She'd compromised his sword's integrity before, and as she swung at the notch in the blade, it shattered halfway up.

She winced against the flying splinters, but the guard hesitated longer. As he dropped the weapon and scrambled to draw the knife at his belt, she buffeted aside his shield and drove her sword through his neck. Blood spurted over her sword and hand. The tendrils stilled in the man's eyes as he slumped to the ground.

After a glance to ensure Garin and the Ilthasi fared well, Wren turned to the felled warrior. She had been dragging herself across the ground in an attempt to flee but stopped and held up a weaponless hand as Wren stalked toward her.

"Mercy!" the guard gasped as Wren stood over her. "Please, have mercy!"

"Why?" Wren itched to end it. "When have you shown us mercy?"

"Please... I don't want to die."

Wren positioned herself for the strike and raised her sword. "None of us do."

"Wren!"

She grimaced and looked up. Garin stood a dozen paces away, his battle concluded. Sorcery had been his friend, as it ever was; he had twisted her roots around one guard to crush them, while the other had succumbed to flames. Horror shone from his eyes.

Snarling, Wren flicked her blade at the guard. The woman winced as blood speckled her face.

"Thank your stars he was here," Wren said before turning away.

Garin hovered next to Wren, then moved to the fallen guard. She listened to the sounds of him binding their hostage with sorcerous vines, a familiar task throughout the war. All the while, she could only breathe. It did little to settle her racing heart.

Wren raised her hand and stared at the blood drying on her glove.

When she'd first insisted on being trained in combat back in Halenhol, her father had sighed. *Know the path you walk, Daughter,* he'd said. *I've seen many men go down it and not return, Tal Harrenfel included. Fight too long and the war begins to live within you.*

As in so many things, Falcon Sunstring had seen it true. All her life, she'd striven against tyrants and villains. She wasn't sure who she was without the war.

No worries on that front, she thought. *There'll always be more bastards needing to bleed.*

If today was any sign, she'd always be willing to bleed them.

Wren clenched her hand into a fist, then turned to Garin. He had been watching her, a somber expression on his face but looked away as their eyes met. He glanced toward the lift, where the Ilthasi had killed the Lathniel archers, though not before the platform had been cut loose. Garin then looked at their bound captive.

"So long as the others were successful," he said without

looking up, "then the false queen is confined to House Lathniel. Take that, and Elendol will finally be free."

And the war over. Neither dared speak the words. No need to tempt fate.

"We'd best report to our queen." Wren nodded at the guard. "You don't expect me to carry her, do you?"

Garin smiled, but it looked as strained as she felt. "I have it."

Raising a hand to their captive, he murmured some words in the Darktongue, the iteration of the Worldtongue he used for sorcery. The bound woman rose into the air to hover a few feet above the ground.

Wren turned away, recognizing the spell. They'd used the same one to transport the body of Helnor Venaliel, the queen's brother, away from the dragon-burned ashes of Haudden.

Dead gods, all this slaughter.

"Come on," she said over her shoulder. "Don't want to keep Ashelia waiting."

Without a glance back, she led the way back to House Venaliel.

3
CROWNLESS

Garin brushed a hand through his matted hair once more as they stood before the door.

"It's just Ashelia," Wren said at his elbow, her tone more cutting than usual. "She's seen us in worse states."

Ignoring her tone, he raised his hand to the wood, then paused and cocked his head. He was used to disparate sounds from the Worldsong, but the faint notes he caught had a different source. He knew the voice accompanying the plucking of the lutestrings.

Rolan, he thought with a smile.

Wren heard the playing as well, for she snorted a laugh. "You'd think he'd have better things to do than sit and sing."

"An odd sentiment coming from a bard's daughter."

Not wishing to bicker, Garin turned back to the door. The quiet walk to the kintree had cooled his feelings enough to pretend all was well with Wren. He could look at her and see the woman he'd known and loved for the past seven years. She had changed, to be sure: her wiry beauty had blossomed with maturity, her ungainly adolescence morphed into a warrior's prowess.

Yet more than her muscles had hardened. Her scars went

deeper than flesh. Grief for her father's passing had burrowed into her heart, leaving a hole that hadn't closed. Her creased brow was a window to the worrying state of her soul.

Most concerning of all was her song. To a Listener of the Worldsong such as he, every living being had their own song. Hers had once been full of laughter and effortful labor, replete with the need to prove herself.

But through the past five years, war had become the only tune he heard: clashing swords, banging shields, burning homes. The Wren he'd once known would have always taken mercy on those begging for it.

He wondered if she had any mercy left.

"You alright?" Wren murmured. Had it been anyone else, he would have thought there was a note of fear in her voice.

Garin shook the image away and flashed a smile over his shoulder. "Fine."

Facing forward, he knocked thrice. At once, an authoritative if weary voice answered.

"Enter."

Garin pressed open the door. The space beyond scarcely resembled the war room and audience chamber it acted as. From the vine-draped bed to the gentle glow of the werelight lamps to the shrine dedicated to their fallen comrades in the corner, it had a feeling of being lived in. Yet the mounted armor, an enchanted set of petrified bark in the style of Gladelysh warders, and the weapon rack holding a shield and sword next to it were reminders that times had drastically changed for the elves of Elendol.

In the far corner before the mounted armor sat Ashelia. Several attendants stood around her. A pile of missives, half of them opened, lay on a round wooden table shaped like a toadstool. She didn't look up at their entrance but continued scanning the note in her hand for several moments before writing a few lines on a fresh piece of parchment in a flowing script.

Garin watched as she worked. Though she was older than

his mother, perhaps even older than his grandparents, had they still lived, Ashelia remained as timeless and captivating as ever. It wasn't only the unaging aspect of elves, nor that she remained untouched by the war. Far from it—while a single grief haunted Wren, Ashelia carried a thousand. Year after year, she had lost her kin, those befriended over long decades. All for the sake of killing fellow Gladelysh.

She bore a nation's grief.

Though such a burden was too heavy for anyone, Ashelia remained unbowed. Her song was strong and free of the callousness that he heard in Wren's. Her posture was ever upright, her chin lifted. Her clothes, suited for the war she found herself in, and her tightly braided, black hair was kept immaculate and tidy. Her eyes, silver on gray, were ever-brewing storms, only breaking into rain when the moment called for it.

In the course of the civil war, Ashelia Venaliel had become more to Garin than an old friend. She had become his leader. His guide.

His Crownless Queen.

Though he wasn't Gladelysh, he had devoted himself to Gladelyl's cause. It wasn't only because of conviction, but for her and her vision. To free this verdant forest from the lingering touch of the foul Whispering Gods.

He would see her mission through to its end. Even if he had to give his life for it.

Finishing her note, Ashelia set down her quill and handed the message to an attendant. After a murmured order, she cast her gaze over the rest of the gathered. "Please, leave us."

They bowed, their hands moving in circles as elven tradition bade, before streaming past Garin and Wren.

"My friends." Ashelia rose with a smile, eyes taking in their battle-spattered appearances. Garin didn't doubt she noted every cut their opponents had carved on their bodies. "Can I tend to your wounds?"

"They're shallow, Your Eminence. Ashelia," he corrected himself with a sheepish grin, remembering too late her preference while they were in private.

Exasperation touched her expression, but Ashelia made no comment. "Be sure to clean them soon," she said. "We cannot have our finest succumbing to infection."

Garin bowed his head. Though she spoke in a motherly manner, the suggestion was a command coming from the queen's lips.

Wren sniffed. "Do you want our report?"

Ashelia, far from annoyed, seemed grateful for the familiarity. "Please. You were successful?"

"Yes." Wren flashed a smile. "Maone is cut off. Her kintree is surrounded. The damned Lathnieli have nowhere to run."

"We took down eighteen Lathniel men and women," Garin added. "Took one captive as well. And their lift is severed. If they wish to leave their kintree, they'll have to build bridges first."

"Well done, both of you. The other detachments have given similar reports." A shadow of weariness crossed Ashelia's features. "Only the kintree remains."

"Let them rot in it," Wren sneered. "They'll starve, eventually."

"I would like to agree, if only to prevent further loss of life. However…" The queen turned to Garin. "I fear something troubling stirs at the heart of House Lathniel. It is a… disquiet all my mages share."

"Disquiet?" Garin queried. "What do you mean?"

"Can you not hear it, Listener, in that Worldsong of yours?"

At her prompting, he concentrated on it. Opening himself to the Worldsong, he let it flow through him, observing each strain. Since the war began, it had been imbalanced in Elendol, the softer sounds of ordinary lives overwhelmed by notes of violence and motifs of slaughter. The discomfort of listening to it had made him less attentive to its subtler tonal shifts.

Only now did he hear what Ashelia meant. The Worldsong was supposed to be filled with every sound across Aolas, yet as he listened, part of it held only... silence. The emptiness grew to fill his mind, deadening the rest of the clamor.

Garin grew cold as he beheld it. To a Listener such as him, it was like staring down an unending chasm, fearful of falling in.

"What is it?" he murmured.

Ashelia's gaze lingered on Garin a moment longer. "We cannot be certain without investigation. Before now, I wasn't even certain the problem was real. But you heard it, did you not, Garin?"

"Yes." His throat had gone dry so that he had to clear it before continuing. "Or rather, I *didn't* hear it. Where there should be song, there's... nothing."

"Nothing," Wren repeated. "Right. Clear as mud."

"It does tell us one thing," Ashelia said. "We cannot wait out Maone Lathniel. Whatever she plots may prove perilous for Elendol. For the sake of my people, we must end this war." Her eyes flickered between them. "Once more, my friends, I'm pressed to ask the impossible of you. Find a way inside House Lathniel, one that spills as little blood as possible. Help me put a stop to Maone's mischief before she causes more harm. You may rest first, of course," she added, eyes noting their bedraggled state. "But first light tomorrow would be best."

"Of course, Your—Ashelia." With a sheepish smile, Garin bowed and led the way out. Wren shook her head with a tolerant grin. Yet his thoughts were far more somber.

What are you scheming, Maone? How else will you hurt your home?

4

BRIGHT

The dirge had lodged in his head, irritating as a splinter beneath the skin.

Rolan hummed as he descended the winding stairs of his home, sifting all the songs he knew for its identity. One of Falcon's old requiems? A Gladelysh funereal march? Perhaps something he had heard while traveling through the East? It was soft and mournful, its tempo slow, yet somehow, it contained an irrepressible urgency.

"Where's a bard when you need one?" he muttered.

Night had visited a deeper darkness upon Elendol. The werelights suspended around the kintree had cooled and dimmed. He had spent the evening high above, climbing into the upper boughs to pluck at his lute and sing half-formed sentences, yet it had been far from restful.

For months, he'd been trying to capture the civil war his people suffered through in verse. Every attempt ended in frustration. This needling, disconnected song was only the latest interference. Each time he imagined Falcon Sunstring listening to it, he could only picture the deceased Court Bard clucking his tongue.

Too rote, he might have critiqued it. *Too... overdone. An event such as this, witnessed with your own eyes? You must ground it in perspective, dear boy, for it to have any grandeur. What does it mean to* you?

Perhaps that was his problem: he didn't know what he thought. The war had been happening around him for the past five years. He'd seen its horrors secondhand but never up close. His mother had kept him out of it, ignoring his protests to be included. He hadn't been practicing the Dance of the Blade since he was a child only to be set to the side while his people bled and died. Though not yet of age among elfkind, at eighteen springs, he was three years past when Garin and Wren set out on their quest and fought Nightkin, dragons, and immortal sorcerers.

Yet the Crownless Queen had spoken. And even for her son —*especially* for her son—her word was law.

That didn't stop him from making alternate plans.

Maybe I have to see it up close. The idea had taken root as soon as he had it. If a story needed a touch of the personal to make it soar, then Rolan had to bear witness. Experience the war he'd only seen from afar.

And if he had his way, he'd join the fight.

Nearing his mother's door, his nerves were enough to banish the mournful song stuck in his head. But he had scarcely concocted a coherent proposal when a tiny figure at the door sent it skittering from his thoughts.

"Now, now, little monkey," he said in hushed singsong as he approached. "Are we eavesdropping where we shouldn't?"

Kaleras Venaliel looked up with scant shame or surprise. Though only five springs old, he possessed a perceptiveness that went beyond his age. Rare was the time he'd been able to sneak up on his little brother and scare him, try as he might.

"I want to see *Momua*," the boy confessed, gaze traveling back to the cracked door.

"Why? Couldn't you sleep?"

Kaleras shook his head.

Rolan crouched next to his brother and peered intently into his eyes. "Was it the scary noises again?"

The boy hesitated, then nodded. Of late, he had suffered nightmares that seemed largely composed of frightening sounds. Neither Rolan nor their mother could extract more from Kaleras than that.

"Come here." Putting his arm around his younger brother, Rolan whispered in his ear. "Can I tell you a secret?"

Kaleras nodded again.

"Sometimes, I think about things that scare me, too." His mind traveled back to the dirge, though he hadn't thought it had frightened him before. Captivated and distracted him, certainly, but what cause had he to fear a song?

"But I like sleep," Rolan continued. "When you sleep, you feel good, don't you? And don't just nod or your head might fall off."

Kaleras giggled, then whispered, "I like sleep."

"Then how about this." Rolan glanced at the door to their mother's bedchamber. He had only to listen a moment to recognize Garin and Wren's voices. Once more, they shut him out of their confidence. All he could do was stifle his jealousy and turn back to his brother. "We'll go back to your room and I'll play something to help you rest. How's that sound?"

The boy hesitated, then asked, "Can you play a song about my father?"

A pang struck him at the reminder. Less from missing Tal— the years had dulled that pain—but from knowing Kaleras would never know his father.

"Of course," Rolan said. "Come on, down we go."

He had barely risen when footsteps sounded from within the chamber and voices came closer. Unsure whether to flee or open the door first, Rolan found himself rooted in place until the door swung open.

Garin and Wren stood in the doorway. His friends had changed much in the years since they traveled together. Those wrought upon Garin were the more pronounced. Brown stubble spread across his chin and light crinkles formed in the corners of his eyes. Already tall, he'd grown taller still and broad as well, despite being more often at his books in his scant leisure time than practicing the sword, as Wren did.

Yet his maturation went beyond the physical. He'd grown graver, his curiosity dimmed. The innocence left after challenging Yuldor and the Whispering Gods had withered. Perhaps it had begun with their friends' deaths. Uncle Helnor. Falcon. Tal. Ilvuan, the dragon with whom Garin had shared his body and spirit.

The young man walked with solitude wrapped around him like a cloak. A feeling with which Rolan could easily identify.

Despite that, his smile was warm as he faced the Venaliel boys. While Wren started and cursed with alarm, Garin didn't look surprised. No doubt his Worldsong had alerted him to their presence before they came into view.

"Dead gods, Rolan," the young woman exclaimed, punching his shoulder lightly. She'd grown taller, but so had Rolan. Having inherited his uncle's height, he stood several inches higher. "What are you lurking out here for?"

"Heard you playing when we arrived," Garin said before Rolan could think of a response. "Was that a new song?"

Doubly caught off balance, he scrambled to patch himself back together. "Ah, yes. Or it will be when it's finished."

"Father would be proud." Wren smiled, but her gaze grew distant. Rolan wondered if her grief came back to life at the thought. Or did she doubt that Falcon Sunstring would be proud of his daughter as well?

"And you." Garin crouched before Kaleras. "Isn't it late to be scampering about the tree?"

Kaleras smiled and ducked his head. "I couldn't sleep."

"Well, we can't have that. Young princes need their rest."

The doorway darkened again as Rolan's mother emerged from the room. "What do we have here?" she said, her face lifting as she took in her sons. "I've told you, no reunions without me."

Stepping between Garin and Wren, she scooped up her youngest into her arms. Kaleras didn't like being picked up around strangers, but he settled before Garin and Wren, having known them for the entirety of his brief life.

"He was having trouble sleeping," Rolan explained.

"Not the night noises?" Her brow creased. "Would you like to sleep with me, little monkey?"

Kaleras bobbed his head before tucking against her chest.

"Alright, then." She gave Wren and Garin meaningful looks before turning to Rolan. "You should get some rest."

"I will. But could I have a word first, Mother?"

She scrutinized him, then nodded and turned back inside her room. Garin and Wren murmured their farewells before descending to their shared quarters.

Rolan entered his mother's bedchamber and closed the door softly behind him. Drawing in a breath, he turned and faced her, waiting until she settled Kaleras into her bed, then glided back to stand before him.

"What is it, Rolan?" his mother murmured. Her spinning silver tendrils betrayed her apprehension.

He hesitated, still unsure of how to phrase his request. But with her before him, all he could do was forge ahead.

"I heard the news. That the Lathnieli are trapped."

Her lips pinched together. He didn't doubt their shared connection to the House were on both their minds. How could it be otherwise when Rolan's father was among those trapped?

He betrayed you, he reminded himself. *Betrayed all of us.*

Pushing it from his mind, he continued, "When Aunt—I mean, when Peer Maone is brought to justice, I... I want to be there. As a Gladelysh," he hurried to add as his mother opened her mouth to speak. "And as a bard."

"Rolan..." The queen glanced at the bed where Kaleras shifted under the covers. "It isn't safe."

"I don't care." Feeling his temper rising, he forced his voice lower. "I've been through worse and at a younger age. Please, *Momua*. I need to experience it."

"Why? What do you hope to gain?"

Thoughts of Falcon flashed through his mind, as did the chords of his unfinished song. "It's the end of the war. How can I write about it if I never see it?"

His mother peered at him. Her tendrils' whirling slowed.

"We'll see," she said at last. "I cannot promise anything, but I'll consider it."

Rolan clenched his jaw. It wasn't enough. He knew, when it came down to it, what she would decide.

"Mother," he said, trying to sound reasonable, "I know you want to protect me, especially when you put me in danger before. Not by your choice," he added at her pained expression. "But you cannot coddle me because you feel guilty."

"It's not coddling to keep you alive." Instead of softening to his suggestions, she seemed to harden. "I'm sorry, Rolan. If you need an answer now, then it's no. You can come as far as the nearest platform, but no farther. Understand?"

Resentment simmered in him, feeling as if it would gnaw through his organs. He had no choice but to swallow it down and nod.

"Fine." Without saying goodnight, he turned and stalked from the room.

Outside, he regretted his abrupt departure, but his pride wouldn't allow him to turn back inside. Tucking his lute tighter under his arm, he sighed and headed down the stairs toward his room.

Ashelia Venaliel might be a queen, but he refused to let her have the last say. He would find a way in.

Then, at last, he might write a song even Falcon would envy.

5

BURN

"Burn them."

Once, Wren's suggestion would have horrified Garin. Now, he only gave her a long-suffering glance.

"Won't work," he murmured. "We'd need another Heyl to eat through its protections, and I don't reckon we ought to summon a fire devil again, do you?"

Wren only grunted.

He focused on their mission. They were too high to smell the swamp spread out around the roots of the kintrees, but the sulfuric stench of sorcery hung thick in the air. In the distance sounded the churn of the Ildinfor as the waterfall cascaded into the Sanguine River, then the gentler rush of the current as it wended through the lower city of Elendol.

Darkness spread before them, lifted only by patches of light along the giant tree across the gap. They'd stared often enough at House Lathniel that he suspected he'd see nothing new now. But what choice did they have? Fail to take their enemy's kintree and the war would never end. Or it might end in a way none of them could foretell.

Silence, I'm tired of war.

Crouching deeper into the foliage of the branch, shifting so a knob didn't burrow so hard into his belly, he looked up and down the trunk. The last of the Lathnieli had barricaded themselves within the living fortress. The bridges that hung between the other kintrees of Elendol had been severed. The lifts that used to ferry up supplies from the swampy depths of the city were cut and inoperable.

The prospects of an invasion looked poor, and even saying that much was being generous.

"Are you seeing something I'm not?" Wren whispered next to him. The branch they huddled against was wide enough for them to lie side by side. "Because it looks like a death trap to me."

"Much the same," he admitted. "We can't climb, not without getting slaughtered before we get to the lower branches. Can't erect bridges while the guards keep watch."

Wren huffed. "Then that leaves flying. Where's your dragon when you need him?"

As her eyes darted to him, he tried not to let it show how her remark stung. Seven years it had been since that day atop Ikvaldar. Seven years since they lost Ilvuan while dethroning Yuldor and the false gods behind him.

And lost Tal to them as well.

He pulled his thoughts away. It was easier than it once had been. But as the poets claimed, time had been a salve. The wounds hadn't faded, but they'd scabbed and scarred over. Now wasn't the time to break them open.

An idea served as a distraction. Twisting his head up to stare through the dense forest canopy, Garin squinted at the high boughs of the Venaliel home, judging their height, their sturdiness, their navigability.

"Fly..." he muttered under his breath.

"What's that?"

He shook his head. "Might be nothing. But I think—"

A harsh screech was his only warning.

Garin yanked Wren back as small branches snapped around

them. He felt the rush of compressed air, sharp against his skin even as it passed harmlessly by. The ripped leaves and torn vines demonstrated how much damage it could have done.

Wind arrows. Shot by a Lathniel mage, they carried enough force to kill a careless scout. Only Garin being a Listener, one who could hear sorcery on the Worldsong, had saved them.

"Come on!" he hissed, pulling at Wren's arm. "Before they improve their aim."

She needed no further prompting. Like serpents sighted by a gryphon, they slithered back down the branch to safety.

Aelyn Belnuure stared at Garin, bronze tendrils blazing in his eyes. "We're to understand you have a plan."

Garin pulled his hand away from his arm, where he'd absently touched the scrapes gathered during their scouting mission. It wouldn't do to convey uncertainty when presenting this plan, particularly while surrounded by some of the most eminent elves in Elendol.

"I do," he said. "Though Wren gave me the idea."

"As a jape," she muttered, not looking up as she picked her nails.

"To gain passage into House Lathniel," Aelyn continued.

"It's where we'd like to go, isn't it?"

The mage acted as if he hadn't heard Garin. "The place we've determined to be impenetrable by any power we presently possess. *That* kintree?"

"*Belosi*, please," Ashelia murmured. "Let him finish."

The mage grimaced, but before the Crownless Queen, even Aelyn Belnuure didn't remain unreasonable for long. Now that Ashelia had laid claim to the throne, Aelyn was as respectful to her as he always had been to Geminia Elendola, Gladelyl's late queen. In every other respect as well, the mage remained unchanged since their days spent journeying together. He wore the same wide-brimmed, much-mended hat and kept his black hair in a long braid thrown over one shoulder. His brow was furrowed with a scowl and his eyes ablaze with irritation. If anything, he was more cantankerous than ever, and he'd never been cheerful.

"Thank you, Your Eminence," Garin said.

She turned a long-suffering look on him, but with her Ilthasi captain and Prime Warder in attendance, she didn't contradict his use of her title. "Continue, Ivasaer."

He hid his amusement at her returned barb. Just as the elves had once given Tal a name to commemorate his deeds, so had Garin been named for his role in bringing down the false gods.

Ivasaer. Godkiller.

Not subtle, are they?

He would have been lying to say he wasn't flattered. More importantly, it seemed to confer authority upon him, a thing he sorely needed as a young human in the elven queendom. When he spoke, people listened, even when lives were at stake. Perhaps especially then.

And here he meant to suggest a plan that would fly in the face of that confidence.

Garin scanned the others. Wren, Aelyn, Rolan, who had wriggled his way into the conference—all looked apprehensive, but he knew they would listen to him. The boy thrumming his older brother's lute looked receptive, but the confidence of Kaleras could hardly be called an encouraging sign.

It was the queen and her close councilors he worried about more. On her right sat the Ilthasi captain, Prendyn Agarae, who had lost his persistent smile during the years of civil war along with most of his hair. He watched Garin warily, as if not daring to raise his hopes that there might be an end to the fighting. His clothes were as dark as his disposition, a match for the agents he commanded in their subtler war of subterfuge and attrition.

To her left was an even tougher man to impress. Prime Warder Elidyr Ymalis was as handsome as the captain was unlovely. Hair so bright it was almost white hung in a silken curtain down to his shoulders. His ornate bark armor, once kept pristine, had many marks and divots worked into it. Though he smiled, Garin had long ago learned to distrust it. Poison could fling from that tongue as easily as praise.

Garin listened to the discordant beauty of the Worldsong intermingling with Kaleras's plucked lute strings and gathered his thoughts. He drew in a breath, wishing he could draw in courage with it.

"They're guarding the trunk, of course," he started. "The lifts are cut. We'd be massacred if we attempted to climb. The same goes for erecting bridges across—we cannot hope to grow them while they remain vigilant."

"We're aware of all the ways we cannot approach." Aelyn's upper lip curled. "Or are you merely delaying?"

Garin flashed him a wan smile. "I thought you admired attention to detail."

"I also value my time."

"Aelyn," Ashelia said, warning in her voice.

As the mage sat back with a scowl, Garin continued. "That leaves only one approach untested: coming in from above."

For a moment, even Aelyn was silent. Then the room burst into objections.

"What do you mean, 'above'?" Captain Prendyn asked.

Rolan looked puzzled. "Do you mean to fly?"

"I tried to tell him," Wren muttered, slouching in her chair. "But you know how he is."

Prime Elidyr only smiled.

Aelyn shook his head in mock surprise. "Garin Dunford, I knew you were a fool like your mentor, but you're a damn sight farther than even him."

Before their protests, Garin remained impassive, the Worldsong steadying his resolve. Only once his companions quieted did he speak, turning to Aelyn as he did. "Do you not understand? Or need I 'spell' it out for you?"

For a beat, he saw only the same disdain as before. Then understanding spun the elf's tendrils faster.

"Ah. I see. No, no, it's plain enough." A smile alighted on Aelyn's lips. "From above it is."

6
ABOVE

"*Nyns kaldis fend.*"

A shiver ran through Wren as the spell fueled itself on her energy. She waited, counting to three, before opening her eyes.

It wasn't the first time she'd used the heatvision spell, but she never grew used to it. As it took hold, the world became painted afresh in sunset hues. The branch on which she stood had gathered a rosy tint while the werelight lamps on the kintree across the gap had become a blinding violet-white. Garin and the other eight invaders she stood with—Ilthasi all—were a shade near to an angry bruise.

Wren resisted the urge to scrub at her eyes as they prickled from the spell and turned to Garin. His face glowed, obscuring his features. His eyes were mere shallow impressions, a slight circle around them where the temperature fluctuated.

"What's stopping those guards from using this spell?" She spoke in a whisper, though the incantation of silence Aelyn had erected around them would mask any sounds they made.

She saw enough of Garin's face to notice his smile as he tapped a finger next to his eyes. "The itching."

Wren snorted a quiet laugh. "Probably true."

"Truthfully, I doubt they would bother with heatvision. Unless they had good reason, they wouldn't want to expend unnecessary energy and resources. If they did use it, though, they would have extinguished the werelight lamps or been blinded."

Wren nodded, searching up and down the gloom-veiled kintree for further signs of danger. She clenched her jaw and set a hand to her sword's pommel as she turned back to Garin.

"Well, let's get on with it."

He nodded, then motioned to Aelyn. Though a human and comparatively inexperienced, Ashelia had placed Garin in charge of the infiltration, and not only because it was his plan. As poor as her grasp on sorcery was, even Wren could feel how the world bent to his will. She couldn't hear the Worldsong, but she knew it was there all the same.

Power wouldn't stop a knife in the back, though. Wherever he went, Wren had to be there to guard him.

Besides, we can't let him have all the fun.

Now that it had come to the operation, Aelyn wasted no time on squabbling, though that didn't stop him from scowling, an expression apparent even through her heatvision. Turning to the dozen elven mages gathered behind him—half of those still able and willing to fight—he started issuing rapid commands.

Beyond them, out of sight of them and their enemy, waited Ashelia with Captain Prendyn, Prime Elidyr, and the rest of her soldiers. Ready for the impending invasion.

It all hinged on their mission.

"Up we go." Garin turned up the branch, and Wren followed him. The Ilthasi came after.

With their focus on honing their vision, they had to climb the branches without sorcery—all but for Garin. Among their company, only he had the magical mastery to maintain multiple spells, and he wasn't shy in flaunting it. Garin cast a spell to make his feet and hands stick to the bark upon command, making it nigh impossible for him to fall and allowing him to quicken his pace.

It was a good thing he did, or Wren and the others would have left him behind. The Ilthasi, born among the boughs of the tree city, navigated them without trouble. Wren had become competent at it herself, her natural balance and honed strength proving vital. At night, though, with her vision turned inside out, the going proved slower.

Yet seeing the others outpace her only drove her onward. She wasn't about to be outdone by Highkin elves—they lorded her half-blood heritage over her enough as it was. With reckless abandon, she scurried from limb to limb, the branches growing ever thinner beneath them, the holds more precarious.

And this is the safest we'll be tonight. Anticipation was a fire burning through her.

Soon, they were above the highest level of any kintree spread throughout Elendol. Wren even felt a breeze through the canopy, chill with autumn. She breathed it in before focusing back on the task at hand.

Garin clung to his branch as it swayed in the wind. His voice was steadier than his grip. "Time for the gryphon feathers. I've told Aelyn we're in position. On his count, we leap."

Her hand shook as she withdrew the long feather from her sleeve. Around her, the Ilthasi did the same, appearing as calm as if they dove into darkness every day. Tucking her hand out of sight, she hid her own apprehension with a firm jaw.

Aelyn's farspeak spell whispered around her. "Leap on three. Do not hesitate. One…"

Wren scrambled to bunch her legs beneath her. Feather clutched tight in one hand, she balanced with the other.

"Two…"

She focused on the platform where six guards stood or milled about, a hundred paces ahead and half as many below.

No point in noticing the fall three times that to the ground below. It was too late for doubts.

"Three!"

Wren leapt.

As she soared out from the branch, emptiness loomed beneath her. Small branches snagged her hair and clothes, then snapped as she passed through. In moments, she'd cleared the reach of the kintree. Nothing remained to stop her from plummeting below.

But instead of falling, she floated.

Wren clutched the gryphon feather to her chest, though there was scarcely any need. It was as if the sky had lifted its weight from her shoulders, making her as light as a seed on the wind. *Featherlight,* Aelyn had called the spell. It lived up to its name.

Wren stared around with wide eyes, shedding her fear like a snake would its skin. A grin stretched across her face.

Never thought I'd fly.

Wonder couldn't last before necessity. Wren judged the trajectory of her descent. Despite the spell, she kept enough weight that her flight became more of a glide. Twisting around, her stomach jolted as she saw that Garin and the Ilthasi were above her. They'd become lighter than she had, the strength of their mages' spells happening to be stronger than hers.

Just my luck.

Facing forward, Wren drew her sword, nestling her hand under the hilt's gilded basket. Golden runes gleamed faintly in the darkness along the steel. The Origin-forged weapon resembled a rapier, but with a thicker blade suitable for both thrusting and cutting. Fashioned for war, unlike those carried by Highkin elves.

Starbright, she thought, and the enchanted sword sent a thrill of energy pulsing through her.

Her approach hadn't gone unnoticed. On the platform ahead, guards stared in her direction. She muttered a curse as she realized why: soaring in lower made her more visible than her comrades.

The Lathnieli reaching for their weapons made it plain she'd been spotted.

Two guards took up bows, the others drawing blades from their hips. Though every elf could cast a cantrip, none of these seemed to be dedicated mages. Wren bared her teeth and released the heatvision spell. For a moment, the darkness felt suffocating as her eyes adjusted to seeing by the glow of the werelight lamps.

The archers nocked arrows and aimed. She held her blade before her, tongue pressed against the back of her teeth. The railing grew rapidly near, the featherlight spell losing effectiveness the farther she went.

Blight your useless spell, Aelyn! She hoped she'd have the chance to tell the mage in person.

Light flashed on the arrowheads as the guards loosed.

"*Wuld!*" Wren twisted her sword as she summoned wind to toss the missiles off-course. The arrows didn't find their target, but their interference sent her spell-lightened body sailing off course. A mess of branches loomed before her, threatening to batter and entangle her. The balcony was ten paces below, where the guards raised their free hands, preparing to use what sorcery they were capable of. If she stopped or slowed, they would have a simple time picking her off.

She had one path forward. One chance to survive.

Wren released the gryphon feather and plummeted to the balcony.

She nearly fell short. Her feet cushioning the blow, she tumbled against the railing, the shaped wood clapping against her side. As she fell away, Wren managed to wrap an arm around a baluster and cling to it.

The dark forest floor yawned far below.

No time for fear. The guards swung and kicked at the arm holding her up. Spitting and cursing, Wren shoved Starbright into its sheath and withdrew her arm. Climbing along the railing like a treetop monkey, she scrambled to escape. Only as she gained a moment's space did she think of another option.

"*Kald bruin!*"

Flames roared from her outstretched hand and bathed the balcony. The guards shouted and icy mist bloomed as they countered the spell with their own. Her body chilled from the cost of her spell, but she had plenty of heat to spare.

Wren vaulted over the railing, drawing her sword in time to meet the charge. The guards were no dancing masters, but they moved with grace and coordination as they closed in. She barely parried and dodged the initial blows and was hard-pressed to keep up as the following strikes fell.

She'd never been one for idle dancing. She had a poorer ear for music than one raised as a trouper should. But the tempo of battle was a beat she could keep. It wasn't a stiff and stolid rhythm, but one full of erratic notes, false starts, and sharp points. It was wild and evolving, as deadly and precarious as prancing on a knife's edge.

This was the only music that made her feel alive.

Wren feinted a strike, gaining an opening for a quick fire cantrip. As one guard cursed and fell back, a hand held before his blistered face, Wren slashed into the thigh of his comrade, then across his throat as he stumbled. The guard slumped to the ground, dead or dying. She backed up, letting the pair behind him make the first move.

Only as the air hummed did she realize she'd forgotten about the archers.

"*Jolsh heks!*"

A barrier of wind that she hadn't summoned blew up before her, knocking aside the arrows aimed at her head and protecting her from any further ones. Wren jerked back and looked up as someone landed beside her.

She scowled at Garin as he stood. "I had it."

"Sure you did." He turned his eyes meaningfully downward. "Those are shallow, right?"

Wren followed his gaze and blinked. Blood—her blood—seeped through a rip in her leather jerkin. One guard had landed a blow without her realizing it. Even as she noticed, she only felt a dull ache from the wound.

"I'm fine. Don't we have bigger problems?"

Garin flashed her a grin as he drew his sword. Scant as her sorcery was, Wren still felt its ravenous yearning for her power. Instinctively, she stepped away, the railing pressing against her back.

Above, the Ilthasi were descending on the rest of the guards and dispatching them with swords, spells, and knives. Garin dropped his wind shield and jerked his head forward.

"Shall we let Aelyn know he can build the bridge now?"

"You tell him." Wren stalked toward the stairwell that wrapped around the kintree. "I'll scout ahead."

"Don't go too far," he called after her.

She was already turning the corner.

7
KIN

Rolan seethed as he watched the soldiers charge across the bridge.

Under Uncle Aelyn's watchful eye, the mages of the Emerald Tower had extended vines and branches across the chasm to the Lathniel kintree, forming a stout bridge within minutes. At another time, he might have viewed that as a feat deserving of a song.

Falcon Sunstring would have extolled endlessly the significance of the moments he witnessed and the bard's duty to capture and glorify them. But Falcon wasn't here, thanks to the false god these traitors had served.

Traitors he'd once called family.

He bunched his hands into fists. All he could do was stand by and watch as others marched to the battle. He'd belted on his rapier and wore what light armor his mother allowed him, yet she still refused to allow him to fight. The Crownless Queen seemed to have forgotten all those times he'd already come through danger.

He stared after those who marched into the battle. The Ilthasi who had emerged from the dens where they'd hidden upon

Ashelia's return. Guardsmen loyal to House Venaliel and those from allied Houses. Warders called in from the borders. Mages of the Chromatic Towers, Uncle Aelyn included, adopting martial roles ill-suited to their pedantic and scholarly ways. Even some from the Imperial bloodlines, who reviled the fanaticism of the Empire they left and the cult whose thrall it had long been under.

It was a jumbled army, but it had served its purpose. After five years, they had clawed back possession of all but this lone tree.

I have to witness it, he told himself again. *The end of it all.*

His mother stood before him, clad in the bark armor of a warder. Her commanders stood to either side. Ashelia stood as still as a tree as she watched the invasion unfold. Only when the last of her soldiers stepped foot on the bridge did she turn to Prime Elidyr.

"Once we've received word that Peer Maone Lathniel has been apprehended, we will proceed."

"Your Eminence." The Prime Warder bowed his head.

"If I may, Your Eminence," Captain Prendyn murmured from her other side, "I would request that before we enter, my agents signal House Lathniel is cleared of traps or other unpleasant surprises."

"She would not wish to destroy her own kintree." His mother paused before continuing. "Or perhaps she would, to keep it out of my hands. Very well. So long as it does not delay us overlong."

"It will be as you say." The Ilthasi captain closed his eyes. A humming began in Rolan's ears, a sign he'd learned meant sorcery was at play.

Sending messages to his subordinates.

From farther down the enormous tree, Rolan heard the distant sounds of fighting. Their soldiers were making quick progress cutting down the Lathniel guards in their path. Recalling days spent in the bowels of the majestic tree, he knew they would be nearing the banquet hall, where Prime Elidyr expected the greatest resistance awaited them.

Growing restless, Rolan looked to his left. As young as he was, Kaleras stared at the kintree with a furrowed brow, as if he understood the gravity of these events. Seeing such solemnity on his little brother's face compelled him to reach out and ruffle his dark, curly hair.

Kaleras jerked away and glared up at his brother. "Stop!"

"Stop yourself." Rolan nudged him with his hip, tottering the boy a step sideways. "Cheer up. You look far too serious."

"But isn't this bad?" Kaleras's eyes fell to where the fighting was thickest.

"Yes and no. It isn't good when we have to fight. But we're fighting for a good thing."

Surely, it was too fine a distinction for a five-spring child. Yet his little brother, always more perceptive than his years, nodded as if he comprehended.

And perhaps he does.

All the years he'd been alive, Kaleras had lived in war. Perhaps even more influential was his half-blood heritage. No one was biased toward him, yet Gladelysh society was littered with ways the Highkin were casually cruel to those not of "pure" lineage. An observant boy could hardly miss when he was derided or excluded, and no number of explanations could stop that.

A trio coming across the bridge shook him from his thoughts. Rolan narrowed his eyes, trying to pierce the gloom and see who approached. Two of them were Venaliel loyalists, the antlered stor emblazoned on their bark armor.

The one they escorted was as far from loyal as one could be.

Rolan's breath caught before he forced it out in a hiss. *Calm*, he told himself. *Don't let him see.*

Yinin Lathniel stumbled, bound hands clasped before him. Slowly, he raised his gaze first to Kaleras, then up to Rolan.

"Yinin." The Crownless Queen was cold as she addressed her late bond.

"Ashelia." His father's upper lip curled, a tinge of his old pomposity returning. Heat blazed through Rolan's chest at the sight.

"You will address Her Eminence with due courtesy or be removed from her presence," Prime Elidyr warned, steel in his voice.

"Of course. My apologies, *Your Eminence*," Yinin all but sneered. His ire was little reduced as his eyes flickered over Kaleras. Yet as he turned once more to Rolan, his gaze softened. "Rolan. My son."

Rolan stiffened. *Son*. How he despised Yinin's right to that word. He found little to admire in his father. The fastidiousness with which he'd maintained his appearance had given way to greasy slovenliness. Though he still spat poison, he looked far from the resolute rebel. No bruises or injuries marked his flesh, telling of a bloodless surrender. Either Ashelia's rejection or the civil war had ground out all artifice from the man, leaving only this sniveling husk behind.

Yet memories pricked the back of his mind. His father's hands on Rolan's shoulders, tight and sure. The moments when Yinin calling him son felt a thing to be proud of. The rare times his father settled him down to sleep, fingers brushing back his hair.

Possessive. Self-important. Impatient. Even the good memories were run through with holes, taking on water like a sinking ship.

And there was Tal. He recalled the deceased man's laugh, his crooked smile. The way Rolan's mother looked at him. The way he'd protected them both.

Even in their brief time together, Tal had become a father in every way that counted.

Rolan held Yinin's gaze and kept his voice steady. "Yinin."

His birth father recoiled like Rolan had struck him. "So," he said, eyes narrowed, "you'd choose your bitch mother and her *kolfash* bastard over me, boy? *My noble son.*"

Rolan curled his lips in disdain while the guards handled Yinin roughly.

"This is your final warning!" Prime Elidyr stepped toward the prisoner.

"Enough," Ashelia said, sounding tired. She nodded over her shoulder. "Confine him to a room. A small one. I will deal with him later."

The guards bowed, then seized Yinin by the arms. As they passed, Rolan's father moved toward them, only just kept at bay by his handlers.

"You think you've already won, don't you?" His eyes were wide, tendrils swirling with feverish brightness. "Deluded, all of you! You can't win this." His frantic laugh was strangled as his captors jerked him away, but he continued to shout over his shoulder. "You have no *concept* of what you face!"

"Away!" the Crownless Queen ordered, and the guards hauled their captive out of earshot.

Rolan felt little desire to look after his father. Looking down, he noticed Kaleras had turned back, the crease in his brow deepened.

"Don't listen to him, Leras." Playfully, he tweaked the tip of one of his little brother's ears, only a hint shorter and rounder than his own. "What does he know? He's a traitor to the queendom."

"But isn't he your father?"

Rolan hesitated, but only for a moment. "Only in name."

Again, Kaleras nodded as if he understood. His eyes—russet like his father's and silver-threaded like their mother's—stared up at him. "Then we're both fatherless."

"I guess so. Good thing we have each other."

He drew him in close to his side. Kaleras wrapped one small arm around his leg and leaned against him.

A humming started in Rolan's ears, demanding his attention. Captain Prendyn had lowered his head as if listening intently.

"Most of the kintree is secured, Your Eminence," the Ilthasi said a moment later. "Ivasaer and Wren Moonblade have led our forces to the entrance of the banquet hall. Peer Belnuure requests your permission to penetrate its barrier."

"He may proceed," Rolan's mother responded. "But they are to withhold from entering until we join them, so far as that remains possible."

"As you command, Your Eminence."

Excitement and apprehension coursed through Rolan in equal measure. Prying Kaleras's arm from his leg, he stepped forward, drawing the gazes of the queen and her captains. "I'm going with you."

"No, Rolan. Watch over your brother." His mother's eyes flashed a brighter silver, lightning amid storm clouds.

He'd faced enough of her furies not to flinch. "The guards can do that. I want to fight for our home."

"And I've given you my answer. If you will not obey your mother, obey your queen."

He flinched as if struck. She had never wielded her authority against him before, not like that. Yet he understood why she did it. This was war. She wanted to keep him as far from it as she could.

But I'm not a boy any longer.

Rolan nodded and lowered his eyes, hoping he hid the rebellion simmering inside.

His mother seemed satisfied. "Keep them here," she spoke to a guard standing at their back. "And keep them safe. Swiftly, now." This last, Ashelia spoke to her captains before leading them along with her personal guards over the bridge. Only as she made it halfway across did she look back.

Rolan didn't meet her gaze.

He looked up once they'd disappeared from sight. Setting a hand to the hilt of his rapier, Rolan clenched his jaw. It was no small thing to defy his queen mother. But he refused to bend to her will his entire life.

History was being made. It was time Rolan had his own heroic moment.

Bending down, Rolan put himself level with Kaleras. The somber boy held his gaze.

"I'm going in after *Momua*. You stay here, alright?"

"But she told you to stay here, too."

Rolan ruffled his little brother's hair. Kaleras pulled away, tendrils spinning faster.

"We cannot always do what she wants. I have to do this."

"Then I want to go."

"You're too little, Leras. Promise me you'll stay safe here?"

His mouth puckered into a pout, but as Rolan raised an eyebrow, his little brother nodded.

"Your Highness," the guard watching over them said, "I cannot allow you to leave. Her Eminence commanded—"

"She commanded you to keep my brother safe." Rolan rose to his feet. He was taller than the soldier, and though he paled in a comparison of strength, skill could compensate for bulk. His mother and his dancing masters—and Wren as well—had seen to it that he lacked none with a blade. "You cannot do that if you follow me. So you'd best stay here with him."

"Prince Rolan—"

Rolan was already turning on his heel and striding away, heart keeping tempo with the hum of sorcery and the crescendo of battle below.

8
STAND

Garin watched with arms crossed as Aelyn pitted his will against the enchantments of House Lathniel.

A mighty hymn rose from the kintree as it defied the mage and his assistants. Its song was stalwart and deep-rooted, cultivated over centuries to protect its occupants. Even the expertise and efforts of a dozen sorcerers struggled to overcome the barrier it erected before the Lathniel banquet hall.

"You sure you shouldn't help him?" Wren leaned against the railing next to him, taking another bite from an apple she'd looted from the Lathniel larder. She didn't seem bothered by the blood speckling her from foot to face as she chewed on the fruit.

"I offered. But you know how Aelyn is."

"Don't I ever."

Garin looked beyond the translucent barrier. Like the other banquet halls he'd visited, this one extended nearly the full breadth of the kintree. Werelights hung in the air, painting the chamber in scarlet light. The long tables had been turned over in makeshift barricades. Behind them stood its sparse occupants.

Two score, three at most.

It was a pittance of the force the traitor queen had begun with. The years of sustained resistance had worn down House Lathniel's supporters from thousands to these remnants. Most had abandoned the cause rather than be killed. As Ashelia piled on evidence of Maone Lathniel's crimes, many had found it hard to continue supporting her.

Two figures rose above the rest on the central stage. One stood, hand placed on the back of the glittering throne: Jondual Lathniel, Prince Consort and bond to the false queen. Unlike his bond-brother, Yinin, whom Garin had glimpsed being apprehended on his way down, Jondual had kept up his oily appearance. Tight, sleek curls cascaded down his back to his waist. His sharp chin was upturned, his severe lips pressed together. The scarlet robes he wore, threaded through with silver and gold, lacked even a single crease. His eyes remained unshifting upon their adversarial force.

The so-called Rightful Queen sat on the throne. Unlike her spouse, Maone Lathniel had undergone far more changes, few of them for the better. Once, she'd been undeniably beautiful in the way of an elder elm: distinguished, eternal, implacable. Her clothes—lacy, white, and glowing with imbued light—harkened back to elegant years not far gone. The rest of her contrasted those memories. Her eyes were fever-bright, violet curling through the dusky blue like lightning flickering behind storm clouds. Her lips were slightly parted, a predator awaiting its prey. Her skin, rich-dark, had grown ashen and pale. Never had she more resembled her family name of "Graybark."

Worst of all was her song, distinct even among the others gathered. The silence he had heard in the Worldsong was multiplied in her own. As if a part of her had withered and died, like a tree rotting from the center outward.

Something about her reminded Garin of the Extinguished, the immortal sorcerers who had served—and mostly fallen—

with Yuldor. A senescence claimed her not only of the body, but of the soul.

Upon her brow rested the royal crown. Once, Garin had seen it worn by Geminia Elendola, the late Elf Queen. Made of star-white gold that shone with a light even brighter than Maone's dress, it was fashioned in elegant patterns of vines and leaves that looked so fragile it seemed it would break at a touch.

Seeing Maone wearing the crown sent a surprising fury spiraling through him. Wren was more prone to anger than he was, yet here before them were those responsible for all this senseless violence. He scarcely knew what it had been for.

Power? Can that be worth all this?

Aelyn loosed a triumphant cry, bringing Garin's awareness back to the barrier. The enchantments loosed one final screech through the Worldsong, then fell silent. The air before the banquet hall shimmered as the last of the sorcery fizzled away.

Even before the light died, warders had closed around Aelyn and his mages, bark shields raised and braced. Instinct had Garin drawing *Helshax*, his other hand raised to ward off arrows. Wren stood ready at his side, all pretense of leisure discarded along with her half-eaten apple.

But no attacks came from their cornered enemy. Maone didn't even rise from her throne. By all appearances, the false queen was still in control of her fate. Listening to her hollowed song, Garin couldn't repress his doubts any longer.

"Wren. Something's not right. Maone Lathniel sounds… wrong."

She shot him a look. "We have the bitch cornered, Garin. Both the Ilthasi and mages have swept the kintree for traps. We outnumber her thirty to one. What can she possibly do?"

He frowned at the false queen. For a moment, her febrile eyes alighted on him, then moved past, judging him unworthy of her consideration.

"I don't know," he murmured. "That's what frightens me."

Wren shook her head and moved forward, eager for action. Garin had no choice but to follow. As ever, he had to keep her from getting herself killed.

For as long as I still can.

"Hold!" ordered Aelyn from between clenched teeth. Agitation gripped the mage, though he at least had reason for it this time. Wren and Garin stepped up next to their old companion, others shifting to admit them.

"We're still waiting on Ashelia?" Wren sounded miffed, like a royal command was an inconvenience.

Aelyn whipped his head toward them, eyes raking across their faces. "Her *Eminence*," he said with sharp emphasis, "is nearly here. We are to hold our position until she arrives."

Wren ignored the hint. "Garin says there's something wrong with Maone. Maybe we shouldn't give her time to think about what she'd like to do."

To his credit, Aelyn didn't dismiss the concerns, instead narrowing his eyes at the false queen. Only after several moments' study did he speak again.

"Foulness taints her aura. Ah, Maone." A smile curled his lips, mocking and delighted at once. "She has been dabbling in dark things. What, I cannot say. But they have planted deep seeds within her."

Garin had heard the truth of it already, but for Aelyn to echo his concerns made them feel more real.

"Then an invasion might be the wrong approach," he said. "Look at her, Aelyn. Falcon would have called her 'as pleased as a fat cat' or something of the like."

Wren laughed. "Don't leave off adventuring to become a bard, Dunford."

"This is what she wants," Garin continued, ignoring her. "She has a plan to punish us or take back Elendol, I don't know which. But this is the last place Her Eminence should be."

"And would you like to tell her to turn back?" Amusement

spun in Aelyn's eyes. "The Crownless Queen comes. She has commanded us to hold. I will not disobey her."

Garin looked at Wren. She shrugged at his unspoken query. If Ashelia had to be disobeyed, they were prepared to face the consequences. Especially if it meant saving her life.

His attention was brought back to the banquet hall as Maone Lathniel stood. In her hand was a knife, a misshapen thing black and veined with glowing violet. Even an apprentice weaponsmith couldn't have so badly bungled the forging of a weapon.

The song it sang was worse still. Tortured screams. Metal sawing through bone. Blood hissing as it hit fire. A thousand cruelties rose from it. Garin recoiled, wondering what atrocities it had seen and who could be behind such an artifact. It was old, older than the sword he held, older than the gods they had overthrown and the dragons who became their allies.

Old as Aolas itself.

"You wish to overthrow me." Maone's voice was high and parched, but it rang across the chamber. "*Your Rightful Queen!* Was I not the true heiress to Geminia Elendola? Is my inheritance not in keeping with our traditions and the Eternal Laws?"

She pointed the foul blade forward. Garin flinched from it. From the corner of his eye, he saw Aelyn step back, eyes fixed on the artifact. Even Wren frowned.

"But you deemed me unworthy. *Me!*" A laugh screeched from her throat. "When I have done nothing but serve our queendom faithfully. When I have given all I am to keep it whole!"

"You have poisoned it, Peer Lathniel," Aelyn called across the banquet hall. "You have torn it up, root by root."

The false queen shifted the knife to point at the mage. Garin stepped closer to him. Little as he wanted to be under its aim, his spell-devouring sword stood a better chance against any curses than Aelyn's sorcery.

"And you haven't, Aelyn Cloudtouched?" she spat. "You, who

are so fascinated with the dark that you scarcely emerge from it? You are a coward, *Peer Belnuure*. You have not the courage to seize power when it lies before you!"

Aelyn sneered. He understood, as Garin had from the start, that words would do nothing to sway this woman. Whatever evil seeped from that weapon had long ago infected its bearer.

"You believe you have won." A harsh laugh stuttered from the swaying queen. "Oh, how you will suffer, *all* of you! And I, Maone Lathniel, the Undying Queen of Gladelyl, shall rule evermore. Bear witness to the beginning of my eternal reign!"

Garin tensed, readying to meet whatever she sent toward them, but no spell issued from the twisted dagger. Instead, the false queen spun, knife leading—

—and rammed it into her bond's chest.

Prince Jondual staggered beneath the blow, eyes wide with shock. His hands scrabbled over his wife's, then slipped away as his lifeblood spilled freely. Maone watched him die with a stoic expression. She only pulled the knife free as he collapsed to the stage.

"You shall be by my side, my beloved, my bond," she said in a carrying whisper. "Always."

"Mad bitch!" Wren hissed. She looked first to Aelyn, then Garin. "Why's she doing our job for us?"

Garin could barely hear her. The gnashing song issuing from the knife had multiplied a dozen times over. And where Jondual Lathniel had stood, something shimmered in the air, a purple, writhing light beginning to take on a greater form.

"We have to stop her." He murmured the assertion, though he didn't know how to accomplish it. Killing her would be the surest way, but with the false queen's most loyal soldiers and mages occupying the space between, he doubted they could make it in time.

Aelyn ground his teeth loud enough for Garin to hear it over the fell song. "Prepare for battle!" he grated. "Be ready to charge on my command!"

Maone scarcely seemed to notice. She tilted her head back, face lifted to the ceiling, and stared as if seeing things visible only to her. Lifting the knife, she held it with the point facing toward her. Her bond's blood dribbled down her arm, darkening her white garments. Her other hand rose to wrap around the hilt.

"*Eternal!*" she shrieked, then drove the dagger into her chest.

Garin watched, dumbstruck, as the false queen stumbled, then pitched back against her throne. Her head knocked against the enchanted wood but she was beyond noticing. Her hands fell away from the dark hilt. Blood spread like roots across her body.

Why? The question circled through his head. *Why do any of this?*

Yet with her death didn't come the cessation of the murderous dirge, but a crescendo. The air where she'd punctured her chest shimmered with the same dark light as from Jondual, bubbling like an unsettled bog. The aberrations reached toward one another like lovers long absent from their shared embrace.

As they touched, the Worldsong screamed.

Garin reeled, nearly falling to his knees. Only Wren's hand on his arm kept him upright. His vision blurred under the onslaught of sorcerous sound. Never had it sounded like this, even when facing Yuldor and the Whispering Gods.

Squinting, he peered into a darkness deeper than any he'd ever known. One devoid of light. One that swallowed it whole.

From it poured nightmares.

9
DREAD

Wren wrenched Garin back as she studied the enemies gushing from the tear in the world.

Most she'd seen before. Ghouls, decaying pale flesh hanging from wiry bodies, mindless fury writ across skull-like faces. Witikos, towering and lumbering, broad horns topping skeletal, spine-infested forms. Two nekrots, hunched over in stolen, mismatched armor, clutching staves and pulsing with sorcerous command over the other Nightkin.

Then emerged one monster she'd only heard tales of.

It stood at least seven feet tall, its single, curved horn rising a foot higher. All along its body was black armor that seemed attached to its flesh like a beetle's carapace. Between its gray lips, she glimpsed rows of small, sharp teeth crowding out each other, black ichor glistening from where they cut into its own mouth. Its eyes, dark and many-faceted like a fly's, bulged from its armored face. From up and down its back and limbs erupted fins sharp as sword. They weren't its only weapon: in one clawed hand, it carried a longer version of the horn on its head, as if it had ripped it from the skull of a rival.

Yet it wasn't the sight of it alone that made Wren quake.

Sorcery emanated from it in waves, washing over the occupants of the banquet hall. At its first touch, some warriors fled, unable to withstand the mind-numbing terror it spawned. Wren froze, only clinging to Garin by instinct.

Dreadknight, she thought, mind catching on the name like a leaf in a whirlpool. *Dreadknight, dreadknight...*

"Wren! Don't listen to its song! Oh, Yuldor's black balls—*Delsh heks!*"

Warmth enveloped her, body and spirit. At once, her thoughts thawed. Wren shook herself, then blinked over at Garin.

"Mind ward?" she croaked.

He nodded, then looked before them. Wren followed his gaze to see the Lathniel loyalists swiftly being overrun by their false queen's summoning. Soon, the wave of monsters would reach them.

Garin spoke quickly. "I'll try to counter its terror and recover our forces. Can you hold them off?"

She'd released him and moved forward before he finished speaking. "Gladly."

Raising Starbright, Wren watched for her first opponent. A ghoul, working with two others of its kind, tore off an elf warrior's head. It looked up as the body tumbled to the ground, black eyes staring at her through a red-speckled visage. Moving on all fours, it charged, snarling and slavering. Its companions weren't far behind.

As the ghoul flung itself forward, Wren raised a hand. "*Wuld veshk!*"

The creature careened, buffeted back by her wind shield. As the second and third lunged at her, Wren released the spell, whipped her sword around, and dodged to one side. The runes flashed as the blade cut into their faces, gouging cheeks and making more flesh flop loose. Their claws fell short of her jerkin.

The ghouls didn't seem to feel the blows. Slavering for her blood, they rallied and encircled her. The ghoul she'd sent flying back joined them at a sprint.

Wren took in her surroundings. Garin had fallen back, and the other soldiers had run in the terror's wake, leaving a wide space around her. As the ghouls closed in, Wren spun in a circle, sword pointing and spell hand extended.

"*Kald bruin!*"

Blistering flames and an ever-sharp edge sent the nightkin to the ground. As the wounds turned fatal, the monsters would fade into foul vapors. She had only to glance at them to see these were done in.

Wren headed past them to meet the witiko tottering toward her, its massive claws extended, when her eyes caught on the figure still standing on the stage before the portal. The dreadknight had raised its otherworldly sword. Violet light spread over it like veins, then crawled out with the slithering motions of snakes.

Wren fell back before the sorcery, dancing so it didn't touch her feet, but she didn't appear to be its target. Instead, the spell crept over to the ghouls. Like vines over a tree, it twisted around them, then sank into their flesh like roots into the earth.

The ghouls' black eyes glowed aubergine. Then, still threaded through with violet, they rose to all fours and bunched their legs, ready to spring.

"Well shit," she muttered, preparing to meet them.

As the resurrected ghouls threw themselves at her, Wren wove between grasping claws and flailing limbs, parrying and slicing as she went. Clawed fingers peppered the ground as she made free of the frenzied attack, only a few scratches for the worse. None of the ghouls fell, but all three limped, digits missing from their hands and feet. Black blood painted the smooth wood and stained the ornate carpets.

Wren darted a look beyond them. More ghouls came on, scrambling atop the overturned tables. Witikos stepped over the barriers with long strides. The nekrots kept back next to the dreadknight, mouths gnashing as they thrust their staves into the air. The dreadknight itself only watched, its plated face devoid of expression.

She had to kill it. The dreadknight would only bring back the nightkin they cut down. Until he was dealt with, they had no hope of victory.

But how to reach the bastard?

The three ghouls lunged at her, cutting her thoughts short. Behind them came the next wave of monsters. Even if she put down her adversaries, she couldn't hold back the tide.

But that wouldn't keep her from trying.

Wren blasted back a ghoul, then lopped off the head from another. The third crashed into her, claws raking across her body. She worked her blade between them and stabbed it through the gut. As it writhed, Wren thrust her free hand into the wound and hissed, "*Kald!*" then kicked her blade free as it burned from the inside out.

They gave her no time to recover. A line of ghouls sprinted toward her, loping on all fours like the ugliest wolves she'd ever laid eyes on. She sent fire and wind into their midst, but more sprang toward her. Starbright sliced through two, but a third and fourth caught her with hooked claws. Pinning her, they ripped through her enchanted armor and into muscle.

Spitting and cursing, Wren tried to kick them off, but the ghouls were undeterred. As one of them bent down and bit her shoulder, agony spiked through her. She arched her back, screaming.

Her voice was lost in the roar rising behind her.

Hot liquid splattered over her, then both ghouls collapsed atop her. Writhing free of their grips, Wren shoved the bodies off and rose to her knees, panting. Warders and Ilthasi streamed around her, protected at last from the dreadknight's influence and taking the fight back to the nightkin.

A small voice whispered in the back of her head, one that sounded much like her father's. *Fall back. You held. You've done enough. Your deeds will be sung for decades to come.*

She ignored it, rising to her feet and starting forward. She didn't do this for glory or adoration. Hells, she'd be surprised if bards mentioned her in this tale, should any survive for it to be written.

No, she'd been born with the fight in her. And she wouldn't stop fighting until her last breath.

With utter disregard for her wounds, Wren raced forward. The dreadknight—all hinged upon her killing it. But dozens of allies and enemies crowded her way. There was no easy way past them.

But maybe there's a hard one.

A mad idea came to her. A technique she'd only used in practice. But with no other options available, it was time to put it to the test.

Glancing around, Wren saw what she was looking for: a shield, round and spiraled like the rings of a tree trunk, lying next to the corpse of a Lathniel guard. Sheathing Starbright, she gripped the straps in her sword-hand, then raised her head to the stage. The dreadknight was turned toward her, almost as if it watched her alone, though it was impossible to know with his fathomless, faceted eyes.

Watch this, horn-head.

Holding the shield aloft, she set into a run. Dodging bodies, she used a sideways table for leverage to leap into the air, her free hand pointed at the ground.

"*Wuld bruin!*"

She pushed every scrap of will she had into the spell. Her lungs flattened as it extracted its price.

Wind exploded from her palm.

Wren flew across the banquet hall. Below, blood and ichor

A BATTLE BETWEEN BLOOD

sprayed as the combatants injured and slew one another. Unable to draw a breath, she pulled the shield in close to her side. The stage rushed toward her. She braced for the impact.

Pain ratcheted up her body as she crashed into a nekrot.

Both of them tumbled to the ground. Rolling free, Wren wheezed in a breath and staggered to her feet, her free hand bracing against the stage. The wounds across her body yawned wider, blood flowing from them, but she barely felt the pain. Her eyes rose and for a moment, she saw stars. Blinking her vision clear, she came all the way upright.

The dreadknight strode toward her, horn-sword gripped in both of its clawed hands. No mistaking where its gaze fell now. Wren met it with a feral grin.

The nekrot she'd knocked over scrambled away from her, the second one falling back with it. Neither seemed eager to intervene in this duel. That made for even odds—as near as she was going to get.

She made the first move. Raising the shield, she sucked in as deep a breath as she could manage, then grunted, "*Wuld bruin!*" as she released the grip.

Wind battered the back of the shield so hard it shot forward like an arrow. Her aim was true—the tempered wood cracked into the dreadknight's hip, staggering it before ricocheting away.

Wren didn't wait for it to recover. Ripping Starbright free, she dashed across the stage, dodged the fallen bodies of Maone and Jondual Lathniel, and sprang forward with her sword-point leading. The dreadknight moved almost too swiftly to follow, despite how heavy its chitinous armor appeared. Parrying her attack, it nearly scored a counterstroke that would have split her in two.

Stumbling back, she knocked into the throne before recovering her balance. Then she fell into the elven dance Ashelia had taught her, adopting the Form of Water. Until she knew how strong and quick this monstrosity was, it was best to keep to the more balanced of the forms.

To her surprise, the dreadknight moved into a similar stance, matching hers. Its dark eyes caught and held her. They seemed like those belonging to a spider who dreamt of spinning a bug into silk.

She moved first.

Flowing forward, she tested the nightkin's defenses. At first, it seemed to act on instinct, countering at the last moment without grace or form. But as she continued to prod it, its movements grew fluid. Within minutes, the dreadknight was nearly her match.

It learns too damned fast.

She couldn't afford to delay much longer, but to attack too soon could prove fatal. Switching forms, her feet danced atop the hardwood in the Form of Air. Starbright moved from liquid slashes to darting stabs. The dreadknight took mere moments to adopt it. But in those few moments, her sword gouged its chitin, leaving white scores in the armor. Little enough effect, but every armor had its chinks.

The moments between. That was her only chance.

Wren acted on her impromptu plan. Form of Stone—Form of Fire—Form of Water once more. She moved through the Dance of the Blade with all the expertise she'd gained over the years. At each transition, she gained another opening and seized it, battering the places she'd marked the dreadknight before. Most of all, she tried for where the shield had rammed its hip, for it had left a spiderweb of cracks from the impact. With each strike, the cracks opened wider, revealing red flesh beneath.

Only as she moved back to the Form of Air did Wren realize her mistake.

The dreadknight's sword jabbed forward quicker than she could dodge. As she tried spinning out of the way, the sharp end of the horn carved through her side. More than the pain, it was the knowledge that it might slow her that sent fear coursing through her.

A chink in her armor. With that first icy touch, terror came flooding in.

"Yuldor's flaming balls!" Wren gritted her teeth and fell back, trying to stay above the numbing tide. The dreadknight shifted from the Form of Air back to its slow stalk. Either it had grown wary of her or it enjoyed toying with its prey.

Blight me if I let it.

It had learned elven dancing in minutes. She had one last chance to harm the dreadknight. Taking it down was beyond her power: she'd have to leave that to others.

Give them a chance.

She thought of them: Garin, Aelyn, Ashelia, Rolan. All the elves who fought for their home against the monsters still pouring from the rift.

You just have to give them a chance.

The Dance of the Blade wasn't the only technique Wren knew. Dredging up lessons from other tutors over the years, she grasped onto those from the mentor most likely to keep her alive:

Tal Harrenfel.

Wren didn't give herself a moment to doubt. Charging, she closed the distance between them. Her legs felt shaky, her body uncertain, but that only made it easier to move in the unpredictable reel of the lost legend. As Starbright darted against and around the horned blade, the dreadknight tried to learn and counter this new, undefined methodology.

It bought just enough time. Seeing her opening, Wren took it. With a wild scream, she drove her sword into the cracked hip.

The blade pierced through to the hilt. The dreadknight bowed under the strike, yet its arm rose as swiftly as before.

No avoiding this blow.

Wren crumpled. Stunned, she tried to rally and roll away,

but she was quickly losing strength. A crushing kick sent her spinning across the stage. Something soft stopped her roll: Maone's corpse.

She staggered upright and stared. Crackling violet light dominated her vision. Beyond it loomed an unyielding darkness that seized her heart in icy fists.

She never saw the drub that sent her reeling into the rift.

10
RASH

The silencing of her song pierced deep as any nightkin's claws.

"Wren!" Garin cut down the ghoul before him and stumbled back from the line, searching for her. His eyes fell on the tear in reality, still issuing forth its nightmares. He looked beyond them. She had to be fighting the dreadknight still. Foolish as it had been to challenge it on her own, she couldn't have fallen to it.

But the dreadknight stood alone, gleaming dark eyes staring over the melee. A white sword with golden runes, bright amid the black, lodged in the monster's hip.

"*WREN!*"

Their nightmarish enemy had to have sent her through the rift. He hadn't heard dying in her final notes. Even in the chaos dominating the Worldsong, he wouldn't mistake that.

But if she lived, how could she hope to survive whatever lay beyond without her sword?

He needed to reach the portal. Needed to reach *her*. Panic made his hands shake and his legs unsteady. He couldn't lose her. Not now. Not after all they'd suffered through.

Steady, lad, steady. You'll help no one by losing your head.

Tal. His lost mentor spoke in his mind as if he were there beside him, guiding him, as he had so often done in life. It didn't matter if he'd ever spoken those words or if Garin invented them.

The thumping heart of sorcery at the middle of the world had swallowed him, yet Tal Harrenfel remained with him.

Garin wrested back control. Wren needed him. He might not have her brashness to try flying over the battle, but he had other assets. His will remained strong and the Worldsong flowed through him, lending its power to his summonings. He held *Helshax*, whose thirst for sorcery remained unslaked.

It had to be enough.

Garin shoved through the front line of soldiers, sword leading the way. A ghoul leapt toward him, impaling itself on his blade and nearly pitching him back. Teeth gritted, he held back the beast as its struggling lessened, then grew slack on the sword.

He threw up his free hand before the witiko behind could strike with its enormous claws. "*Gef thasht!*"

The Worldsong roared and energy crackled from his hand. Lightning leapt forward, enwrapping a line of nightkin before him. The entire row fell, stunned or slain in an instant. Those around them scattered, holding back the onslaught.

A hint of numbness from the spell crept over him, costing him a moment's delay. Before Garin could speak the next incantation, the dreadknight turned to him. Raising its strange, curved sword into the air, the black blade became engulfed in violet light.

Then it shattered, shards of light shooting into the fallen nightkin, seeding through them. Those that had been corpses rose, doubling their numbers.

The renewed horde pressed forward once more.

Garin fell back with the elves beside him, struggling to calm his thoughts. Destroy them so they wouldn't rise again: that was the only way any of them might survive. Spells leapt to mind, all of them born of fire. Dangerous when fighting in the belly of a kintree.

Do we have any other choice?

He glanced at Aelyn, the mage throwing hexes amidst the nightkin. Aelyn would know what to do once Garin's summoning came.

Turning back, Garin raised his hand and bellowed, "*Keld vorv alak!*"

Ravenous flames leapt from his palm, arcing over the front ranks to descend upon the nightkin. With the hunger and ferocity of a dragon, they devoured one ghoul, then another, then a witiko, moving swiftly and leaving behind only charred bones. The enemies scattered from the hellfire, but the distance wasn't far enough to save them from its murderous clutches. Werelights suspended midair were consumed. The tables, too, caught flame. Not even the walls and floor were spared, sparks beginning to catch.

A gap opened before Garin. Fighting against the shivers brought by the casting, he charged.

His allies shouted from behind, but the Worldsong flowing through him drowned them out. Garin held *Helshax* aloft, and though no nightkin challenged him, it still protected him. Where the flames came close enough to singe hair, the black blade drank in the sorcery, protecting him. He had a clear path to the portal.

The dreadknight stepped before him, blade held in a matching position to his own.

"Yuldor's bloody balls!" Garin skidded to a halt. Sweat streamed down his body and face, and not only from the increasing heat of the banquet hall. He'd seen how it had matched Wren's every stroke. Unlike its minions, the dreadknight didn't appear to fear the flames. If anything, the consuming fire kept away from it, as if afraid of being absorbed in turn.

Yet it's invulnerability was a facade. Wren had injured it.

The dreadknight had extracted her sword from its hip and tossed it to the stage, but the angry red flesh beneath the black chiton shown through still. It was a weakness. A vulnerability to exploit.

Garin raised his left hand. The dreadknight did the same.

"*Thal ovth!*"

Blood boil. Garin couldn't flinch. He threw all his will into imagining the dreadknight's ichor growing molten, cooking him from the inside out. He set his gaze on that wound, using it as his focal point, driving all his sorcery at it.

Helshax's hilt grew icy cold against his gloved hand, so cold he nearly dropped it. It had never reacted to a spell like that before. His enemy's power was unmatched by all but gods and dragons. Gritting his teeth, Garin clung to the sword and pushed harder on his spell, feeding it more of himself and the Worldsong. Despite his numbing hand, his veins prickled with heat. Heat not born of his own body.

The dreadknight stood, untouched by his spell.

Garin let off the casting, heart racing, sword hand aching. The dreadknight lowered its hand as well. Its song filled the room, twisted and haunting.

He knew the truth then: anything he threw at it, this monster could match. The dreadknight was a mimic in both the martial and arcane arts. Yet it couldn't complete a perfect imitation. Wren had harmed it. Its abilities had limits.

Garin couldn't take the time to find them. He didn't need to beat the dreadknight, only move past him. Perhaps, if his spell wasn't aimed at the monster itself, he wouldn't replicate it.

Hoping against hope, Garin steadied his mind, then carefully spoke the words: "*Qed nenik und.*"

In his peripheral vision, he saw them appear: three more Garins, a perfect match to him. Those who could hear the Worldsong would tell the difference in their songs at once, and a keen observer might detect how the illusions didn't disturb the debris scattered over the ground.

Garin didn't mean to give his enemy long enough to notice. At an unspoken command, he and his doppelgangers scattered. One of them charged at the dreadknight while Garin took a diagonal away from its sword hand. He was rewarded with a moment's satisfaction as the nightkin swiped at the charging illusion. As Garin's other self went down, blood spilled from its body and spattered the ground.

He didn't linger to see if the dreadknight would discover his ploy. The rift loomed, blessedly empty of nightkin. This was his opening. None could say what awaited him beyond.

For Wren, he would find out.

Garin took the final steps, then vaulted into darkness.

11
EMINENCE

Ashelia could tell the plan had gone awry even before she turned the last corner to the Lathniel banquet hall.

"Madness!" Captain Prendyn had declared after his Ilthasi agent brought an initial report. "Maone Lathniel has killed herself and her husband to tear open a rift. Nightkin are pouring through!"

She never broke stride. She knew what advice would come next. Prime Elidyr chose to offer it.

"It is not safe for you, Your Eminence. I would advise that you hold back until we can be certain of our next step. I will oversee our troops."

"No, Prime Elidyr," she answered. "We all go. If there is a realm rift in my city, it must be closed at once. Our people have been scarred by too many demons to delay."

Every Gladelyshi remembered the kintrees burned and lives lost to Heyl, the towering fire devil unleashed twice upon Elendol. Thus far, it seemed they would be spared a third appearance. But after five years of civil war, good fortune wasn't something she relied upon.

Tension quivered up her body with every stride, but she kept moving. Her brother was fighting down there, as were her former traveling companions. Her Ilthasi, her warders, and her most loyal subjects all risked their lives to end this hellish conflict.

She wouldn't stand out of harm's way while they died for her. Crownless or not, she was their queen. She would fight for them as hard as they fought for her.

She had never ceased to be a warder. Even more, she was a mother. And a mother did nothing if not protect her children.

As the banquet hall came into view, Ashelia recoiled. The stench hit her first—the stink of sorcery, burnt flesh, of rot and viler substances. Eyes stinging, she calmed her worries to ice and observed dispassionately how they fared.

At first estimation, her forces seemed to hold their own. Their numbers were thinned by a mere dozen. A leaping fire spell, one she recognized as Garin's, had scattered and consumed many of the nightkin. The Lathniel forces lay dead, their corpses scattered across the banquet hall. Aelyn and his mages had erected sorcerous barriers before their own troops, keeping her young friend's deadly hex at bay.

Yet many enemies still stood, and more poured out with every moment. The dark tear atop the stage drew her eye, and not only for the pale ghouls spilling from it. Spreading as wide as she was tall and twice as high, violet energy hissed around the edges, a sign of the sorcery keeping it open. The body of the guilty elf, the false queen against which Ashelia had set herself, became more trampled with every nightkin that emerged.

Maone, what have you done?

A scene playing out before the rift pulled her attention. Fear rose as she saw Garin facing off against the tall black figure clad in insect-like armor from horned head to clawed feet. A dreadknight; Aelyn had spoken of these before, though neither of them had ever had the misfortune to meet one. Gazing upon it, horror seized her chest, freezing her limbs in place. To either side, she felt the captain and Prime Warder stiffen, similarly affected.

But it took more than that to stop one trained within the Chromatic Towers. Whispering a counterspell, Ashelia felt the terror ease its grip. She spread it to the two men beside her and saw them reanimate.

"My gratitude to you, Your Eminence," Prendyn said, shuddering and running his hands over his arms.

Elidyr also nodded his thanks, but his eyes were already hard on the battle, his saber held in one gauntleted hand. "Allow me to lead the charge, my queen. I will gladly rid the world of this monstrosity."

Ashelia already focused back on the duel. As she watched, Garin multiplied, and four different versions of him scattered. An illusion. One Garin charged the dreadknight, only to be cut down in a spray of viscera. Her stomach lurched at the prospect of her friend being cut down.

Then she saw another Garin leap through the rift, and she understood.

Wren. The Ilthasi had reported that the young woman had faced the dreadknight alone and been thrown through the rift. Despite earlier displays of wisdom, Garin was proving as rash as his beloved. The origins of their madness was hardly a mystery.

Ashelia knew better than most how reckless one could be in love.

As the illusory Garins disappeared, she put her young friend from mind. For the moment, he and Wren were on their own. She was the Crownless Queen. Her first duty was to her people.

Save who you can.

Ashelia drew her rapier. Like those she'd gifted to her comrades, she bore an Origin-forged blade glimmering with golden runes. She hoped it would be enough.

"The dreadknight," she said. "He is their commander, the

will behind their army. Kill him and we can put down the others."

Elidyr eyed her weapon. "Your Eminence, I must insist—"

Ashelia silenced him with a gesture. "No time. If you wish to protect me, come along."

Prendyn mopped his shining forehead with a kerchief, then drew the twin daggers sheathed at his hip. "Where you lead, Your Eminence, I'm obliged to follow."

That evoked a fleeting smile. "Pray, don't sound overly enthusiastic."

The Ilthasi captain could only muster a miserable grin.

"Form up!" the Prime Warder shouted to his men. They obeyed at once, mustering to form a gauntlet around Ashelia. She had meant to be at the fore, but grudgingly, she allowed her soldiers to do so. It was as much their duty to protect her as it was hers to protect them.

"Aelyn!" she called to her House-brother, who remained at the front line. Whispering a spell, she amplified her voice to be heard over the others. "*Belosi*, to me!"

Aelyn whipped around, eyes whirling with annoyance. Lips moving in muttered curses, he motioned his mages to fall back toward the end of the gauntlet, lowering their barriers. The hellfire spell was burning out at last. Their path was clear.

"*Forward!*"

The Ilthasi captain and the Prime Warder echoed her command. The company advanced, slowly at first, then swiftly picking up speed. Ashelia ran with the rest of them, feeling her tendrils bright in her eyes, sorcery and blood eagerly leaping within her.

Too long, she'd let others wage her wars. What a relief it was to fight her own battles.

The nightkin let them make it halfway across the banquet hall before assaulting them. Rallying from the edges of the hall and flooding from the stage, they leapt over the fallen to throw themselves on the elves. Warders met them: cutting with sabers, battering with shields, impaling with spears. Aelyn and his mages sent spell after spell into their midst, burning and freezing and blasting them apart. Be they ghoul or witiko or nekrot, none remained in their way.

The dreadknight stepped from the stage to engage them. Then the one monstrosity multiplied into four.

It took her a moment to understand what had happened. Garin's spell—somehow, the nightkin had taken it for his own and replicated it. Before she could yell a warning, Aelyn shrieked the same realization.

"Illusion!"

The warders in front didn't hear it in time. The four dreadknights drove down four nightmarish swords. Before them, three soldiers remained standing, the blades passing harmlessly through. One split in two, the sword severing him from shoulder to hip. His blood sprayed their party and dotted Ashelia's lips.

Spitting, she pointed her rapier at the real dreadknight. "That one! *Take it down!*"

Prime Elidyr moved before her, quick on the heels of the other men. As a small contingent of warders broke off to drive back the nightkin spilling from the rift, the Prime Warder and four of his soldiers engaged the dreadknight. As they fell into various forms, Ashelia was shocked to see the dreadknight take a matching stance.

It knows the Dance.

She pushed against the backs of the warders in front of her, still spreading out under Prendyn's breathless commands. Even if she'd been able to do something, she couldn't reach them in time. The warders attacked in coordination, and some of their sabers landed against their foe, but none left more than shallow marks. The dreadknight was swifter and stronger. Its unnatural blade chopped through shields, armor, and bodies with equal ease.

She moved closer, tailing the other warders who sprang

forward to take the place of their fallen brethren, until a hand wrapped around her arm and jerked her back. Whipping her head around, she stared into the fervent eyes of her House-brother.

"You cannot fight it!" Aelyn hissed. "It will cut you down the same as the others!"

"I have to try, *Belosi*. And you're going to help me."

"Help you die?"

She'd already turned away, assured of his obedience. Even if he hadn't been her brother, she was his queen. Aelyn was nothing if not loyal to the crown.

"After I go in," she called over her shoulder, "I need you to strike it with your most powerful spell. Perhaps the one you used against Heyl?"

Aelyn grimaced, but his hands already rustled through his robes. "You're fortunate I brought the components."

Fortune had nothing to do with it, they both knew. He'd prepared for this moment as thoroughly as she had.

"Aim for where I hit it," Ashelia continued. "I'll try to create an opening."

She started to turn away, but Aelyn's words stopped her. "*Kolesa*, it will replicate the spell. That could be disastrous."

"It's a risk we have to take."

Weapons alone would not fell this fiend. Already, the dread-knight had slain six of her men and injured Elidyr enough to send him stumbling back, a hand held to a gushing wound in his side. Still, the Prime Warder shouted encouragement to his men. They would go bravely to their deaths.

Unless I stop this.

"Now, Aelyn!"

Ashelia charged as she issued the command. Even having kept up her conditioning over the length of the civil war, she felt the weakness that had crept into her body from years out of the fight and bearing two children besides.

She pushed those concerns from mind, pushed away everything but her goal. Here stood the final obstacle between her nation and peace. Safety for her subjects, her friends, her family.

She could not fail.

As she arrived at the warriors ringing the dreadknight, she slowed, looking for her opening. The nightkin moved in the forms with nearly as much grace as a dancing master, pivoting to a new one to match those the warders used against it. Yet there was the slightest hitch as it transitioned between them; almost imperceptible, yet enough to notice and exploit, if she was quick.

Ashelia ghosted onto the stage, trying to avoid the dreadknight's attention. She flinched as it cut down two warders in rapid succession. Still, she bided her time, looking for an opening. Waiting for the moment to strike.

Her eyes fell upon the likeliest point. Upon one hip was a breach in its armor. Red flesh peeked through, and a black fluid thick as mud oozed down its leg. A wound. A place the chitin couldn't block her sword.

The dreadknight pivoted away, then turned back. Its injured hip came into view.

Ashelia snarled as she lunged, rapier leading.

Her aim was true. The point dug into the gap in the armor and bit deep into the red flesh. Only as it came to a sudden stop did she withdraw. The blade had bitten all the way through to the other side of the chitin.

The dreadknight whirled toward her, greatsword leading. Its leg caught with the sudden movement, causing it to stumble and miss, though the blade swept close enough that she felt the bite of the wind, the whistle of air splitting in two.

Ashelia caught her balance and stood before the nightkin, stance ready, rapier half-raised. The dreadknight beheld her with its bug-eyed gaze. It matched her stance, the Form of Water, and advanced.

A shout was the only warning she had as light blazed past her to crash into her enemy.

The beam only lasted a moment, but while it did, Ashelia reeled. The wave of power cascading out made her feel wine-drunk. Staggering, she blinked through dazzled vision at what had become of the dreadknight.

It is enough. It must be enough—

Yet it still stood.

Its chitin had melted where Aelyn's spell had blasted it. The dreadknight leaned to one side. Injured, maybe, but far from fallen.

And in the hand not carrying the horn-sword, an orb of light was pulsing and growing larger.

"Wards!" Ashelia screamed, raising her own. Yet she'd seen the force of that spell. If the dreadknight could fully replicate it, she doubted any of them could survive.

The orb flickered, straining under the force of its own power. The dreadknight raised its hand and flexed its claws.

An arrow flitted through the air, striking it.

Shockwaves battered her. Ashelia rolled across the floor until she thudded to a stop. For a moment, she lay there, stunned senseless. Only by margins did the urgency of the fight crawl back in.

She clawed up into a sitting position, shook her head, and screwed up her eyes at the scene.

The dreadknight had gone down on one knee. The arm that had held the light orb was gone, only a stump remaining. Yet if it felt the pain of its injuries, it gave no sign of it. Even as she watched, the monstrosity rose back to its clawed feet and raised its horn-sword once again.

Someone moved to stand over her. A figure too slight and lightly armored to be a warder. One terribly familiar.

"No," Ashelia moaned, trying to stand. "Rolan, *no!*"

12
SONS

Rolan ignored his mother's pleas as he drew his rapier.

He hadn't planned to face down this creature of darkness and chitin. When he'd drawn his bow, borrowed from those discarded by the warders, he had only meant to protect from a distance.

He'd set his eye to his target. Aimed. Loosed. And, like Mother World herself guided the arrow, he'd pierced the glowing orb held aloft in their dark enemy's hand.

Yet the nightkin lived, and all the warriors, his mother included, were downed. No one stood between the Crownless Queen and her foe. The scene had all the makings of a tragedy poised for the climactic act.

He couldn't stand by and watch his mother die.

Rolan squared off against the armored creature. Leaning on its bizarre sword, a match to the horn atop its head, the nightkin came back to its feet. Even missing an arm and its armor cracked and melted, it stood steady and pulsed with power as it looked down on him. His rapier felt like a twig next to its weapon.

Yet Rolan raised his blade all the same. His moment had

come. Win or lose. Live or die. In this moment, he would be a hero like those he and Falcon had sung of. Like the Court Bard himself had become at the end.

Valor lay not in victory, but in spitting in the face of fate. In sacrificing all for those who meant all to him.

Still, his legs quaked. His sword-arm shook. His bladder strained. Heroism was a more terrifying prospect than he'd expected.

"Fool boy!" someone called from behind. "Get back before you're killed!"

Rolan recognized Uncle Aelyn's voice. The mixture of vitriol and distress in it almost made Rolan smile.

"Apologies, Uncle," he called over his shoulder. "Someone has to stand."

Another familiar voice spoke. "Please, Rolan. Don't do this to me."

His mother's plea nearly broke his resolve. Rolan wavered, the boy in him wanting to obey and believe she knew best. But he was old enough to know that wasn't always the case. That sometimes, she had to be protected from herself.

"I'm sorry, *Momua*, but I must."

He swallowed, his voice breaking. Tears pricked his eyes. The horror advanced on him, raising its greatsword. Nothing would stop the blow from falling.

He remained where he was.

Nearly too fast for him to follow, the sword descended. Rolan leaped aside and tried to parry, but the blow came too hard. The dark creature knocked the rapier from his hand, leaving him scrambling back. He cast a glance over his shoulder to his mother still struggling to rise. His heart sank.

Then it's to be a valiant end.

As the nightkin lumbered closer, he threw forward both hands and shouted, "*Kald bruin!*" Flames cascaded out in a wide plume, enveloping his adversary. He pushed more into the spell, draining his body of heat so he felt as cold as a week-old corpse.

Only as he collapsed did he relent. Rolan panted, his vision spotted. Sorcery had never been his forte, yet he raised his head and blinked through the sparks, hoping the ploy had worked. That his amateur spell had succeeded where all others had failed.

The nightkin was little more than a silhouette to his hazy vision. Yet the flames spiraling around its sword were clear enough as it raised the blade toward him.

"*Stop!*"

A high, childish voice rose, screeching and breaking as if in a tantrum. Chest clenched, breath labored, Rolan pitched around, trying to see where it had come from, then lurching to grab the little person as they darted past him.

"No!" he tried to bellow, but his cry came out weak and breathless. "Get *back* here, Leras!"

Kaleras Venaliel didn't turn. Five springs old and less than half his older brother's height, he stood with a fierceness to match any warder. His towering opponent paused at the boy's appearance, sword half-raised, as if baffled by defiance from such a tiny thing.

The hesitation only lasted a moment. The blazing sword raised to point at the boy.

"*Kaleras!*" their mother screamed. Rolan heard her trying to rise. Sobs broke free of her, hacking and terrible. "Come back to me, *please*!"

The boy ignored them both. Almost, he seemed possessed by a vengeful spirit as he raised his small arms against the nightkin. Believing as only a child could that he could stop the flaming blade, that it would not chop him in two. That he could never die.

Rolan summoned all the will left in him and lunged for his little brother.

He tried to tackle him to the floor, to move him out of the

way or at least shield him with his own body. But he fell short, hands grasping Kaleras's ankles instead. Tugging, Rolan attempted to pull him down. With a little luck, perhaps it would be enough.

Before he could jerk him off his feet, blistering energy shot into him.

Time stopped. Pure, undiluted power flowed through him, *became* him. There was no separation between him and the world—they were one, a continuum, each touching and influencing the other.

The moment shattered.

He pitched onto his back, dazed and breathless. With one hand, he kept hold of Kaleras's foot, but he could do little more than watch.

The world had changed.

Shining lines spun from pure light bisected the smoky chamber. They rooted in Kaleras, in the nightkin, in Rolan himself. Buried into the ceiling, the floor, into every object and individual present. They were omnipresent. Everywhere and in everything.

The Lattice.

Garin had spoken of it: the web of sorcery that permeated the world, unseen by most. With the help of his spirit dragon, Garin had glimpsed it before.

Rolan had never doubted its existence. Yet he was wholly unprepared to behold it with his own eyes.

The sight of it didn't faze Kaleras. His fingers touched upon the threads wending into him as deftly as if he plucked the strings of his older brother's lute. As if they were lutestrings, they vibrated at his touch. A chord, haunting and terribly beautiful, filled Rolan's being.

The threads pulsed brightly. Energy cascaded from Kaleras down them, following their winding path to their dark foe.

Power blasted into the nightkin.

The vision of the Lattice disintegrated. Rolan stared open-mouthed as the horrific being flew back through the air like the hand of a god had slapped it. Its sword fell from its grasp to clatter to the floor, the flames surrounding it extinguishing. The monster itself flew into the rift.

Darkness enveloped it.

Rolan felt a weight lift from his body as the nightkin disappeared. He rose to his knees with a groan, feeling like someone had beaten him with a branch torn from a kintree.

Just in time, he noticed his little brother swaying.

"Leras!" He lunged, catching the boy as he fell. The floor battered him anew, but Rolan scarcely felt it. Cradling Kaleras's limp body, he stared into his slack face. His eyes had rolled into the back of his head, but his chest rose and fell. He was alive.

They both were.

A crazed laugh burst from him. Staring into that small, unconscious face, Rolan ignored the buzzing activity around him, caught in bafflement and wonder.

"What *are* you?" he whispered, the song of this moment composing itself in his head.

13
DUSK

*N*ight fell.

Wren tumbled into darkness. She was blind, senses numbed by pain.

Pain... Did that mean she hadn't passed on to the Quiet Havens? That, somehow, she was still alive?

Yet darkness clung to her eyes, damp and chill. She blinked and brushed a hand across her eyes, hoping that something covered them, that she hadn't gone blind. Or perhaps no light existed in this place, wherever this was.

A soft, sticky substance came away on her fingers.

Gagging, Wren pawed her face and spat. The foul material came off easily, but she felt it clinging to her skin and hair like she'd stepped through a mass of cobwebs.

The sight that greeted her banished all thoughts of discomfort.

A blue orb hung in the sky, painting the landscape in subtle shadows. The land undulated in hills and valleys. It seemed devoid of vegetation but for a purplish plant that spread across the ground. Turning, she found everywhere to be the same except for one place, a break in the bleakness: a tear with writhing purple light around the edges and bright white in the middle.

The rift.

Memories came flooding back. The dreadknight had knocked her through that portal, and none too gently. Wren gingerly touched her wounds and winced. Even with Ashelia's help, they would be difficult to heal.

If she survived that long.

Wren snatched the knife she kept tucked inside a boot and searched for threats. Nothing alarming appeared in the immediate vicinity. For the moment, she was safe.

But where did all those damned nightkin go?

She strained her senses against the gloom. As she breathed in, the stench of the place finally registered—a cloying, acrid decay. Almost, it seemed to rise from the ground itself, or perhaps from whatever spread across it. Wrinkling her nose, she stared at the ground. Not only was it pocked with purple plants, but it had an unnatural feel to it, a springy give like she walked on a mass of toadstools or stepped into rotten wood.

Is this world dying?

There seemed little point in lingering to find out. In falling through the rift, Wren had tumbled down dozens of strides. She turned and hustled back up the incline toward the bright opening, favoring one bruised leg as she went. Her knife, clutched close, she threw a glance over her shoulder, expecting a ghoul's claws to lodge into her back at any moment.

What she caught sight of made her blood run cold.

A bank of fog, thick and pale, came over the rise like a tidal wave. Though its passage appeared gentle, instinctive horror rose in her at the sight.

Wren limped faster, trying to reach the rift first. But she knew she couldn't make it. Hissing with fear and frustration, she spun back just as the mist reached her and swiped with her knife.

Clawed hands formed from the cloud and, despite their

ethereal appearance, they seized her as firmly as corporeal ones.

"No!" she yelled, striking again. "Get off me, damn you!"

Where her blade passed, the arms evaporated into mist, but more only materialized to snatch her. Their touch was frigid, sapping the little strength she had left. Weariness, heavy and implacable, bore her down to the porous ground. All she could see was mist.

Her eyes closed, but still, she lurched about. She sank to her knees, but never stopped fighting. She never would, down to her last breath.

As she sucked down air, the mist forced its way into her mouth.

Gagging, choking, Wren collapsed. Knife discarded, she scrabbled at her throat. There was no stopping the repugnant cloud from working its way inside her. Her limbs went cold, then numb. Her mind went blank. Her hands fell away.

Why fight? What am I fighting for?

All went hazy, indistinct. She fell limp. It was inevitable, this passage. She'd fought long enough.

A light blazed against her closed eyelids.

Sounds came, distant and muffled. Shouts. A familiar voice? She no longer cared. From the darkness spread golden, pillowy clouds far in the distance. Would they catch her if she fell?

Wren tumbled over the edge, eager to find out.

14
ANNIHILATION

"*Wren!*"

Garin fell to his knees and shook her. The foul-smelling cloud had dispersed before the wind barrier he summoned as a dome around them but it lingered at the edges. He couldn't worry about that now.

She was cold to the touch, so cold. Her eyelids fluttered, but her chest, inflated with air, had never expelled its final breath.

He couldn't speculate on what that meant. He would save her. He had to. Glancing up to ensure his barriers held, Garin grasped for every spell he knew. The last he'd seen, she was breathing in this fog. Drawing it out might reverse the effects.

Gritting his teeth, he set a hand before her slightly parted mouth and recalled the last time he'd seen this spell used. Aelyn had performed it on Tal, believing him responsible for his queen's death. Holding the picture in mind, he opened himself to the Worldsong. Even here, far from its origin, it reached through the rift, imbuing him with power. Using it to hold the barrier surrounding them, he separated his mind into two, making room for a second spell.

"*Jolsh roun fith.*"

Wren bucked, back bending upward, mouth falling open.

A BATTLE BETWEEN BLOOD

He flinched at the grotesque sight but clung to both of his castings. Mist appeared, first in thin rivulets, then in a stream, and rose from between her lips. Her chest went flat as he sucked the air out. An orb, barely visible, swirled around her head as a vacuum was established.

Her eyes flew open. Her lips curled in a snarl. He couldn't hear the words she tried to speak, but he could guess.

Let me breathe, you bastard!

With a laugh halfway to a sob, Garin unraveled the spell. Wren collapsed, coughing like she would hack up her innards. Garin kept up the outer barrier as he waited for her to recover.

When at last she could speak, she wheezed, "Showed… your hand, Dunford. Always knew… you wanted to kill me."

"Only when you drive me mad." A tear trickled down his cheek. Garin wiped it away before Wren could notice.

"Saw that." She rose to her feet, using Garin for support.

Pretending not to hear, he took in their surroundings. This realm defied his expectations. It wasn't entirely devoid of light: Thelani, the blue moon of their realm, also rose on this land. More surprising was that nightkin didn't infest every part of it.

Where do the ghouls come from? The witikos? The nekrots and dreadknight?

His eyes strayed to the fog amassing outside the dome of wind. The mist had attacked them. It possessed a sort of sentience, one malevolent toward invaders. Perhaps it had something to do with the nightkin in their realm. Perhaps it was even their source.

"Can you walk?" he asked Wren.

"If it means getting out of here, I'd crawl." She jerked her head toward the rift. "Let's go."

Wren hobbled, favoring one leg. Garin moved to support that side, slinging an arm over his shoulders and hunching down, his frame taller than hers. With the Worldsong only contributing a fraction of its usual power, he was becoming breathless from his sustained spell.

The winded leading the lame. He smiled, hearing Tal's voice speak it in his head. The thought gave him the strength he needed to press on.

The rift came under the dome as he moved it with them. Its strange sorcery teased his mind, distorting the Worldsong and almost undermining their protection. But they were mere steps away. A few more, then they would be back in their realm to deal with the remaining nightkin.

At least we'll be alive.

They reached the rift and set through it. The light became obscured by darkness.

Something crashed into them.

Garin flailed, trying to hold onto Wren and his spell, but he failed at both as he plowed into the ground. Wren cursed and went rolling away.

Scrabbling for his sword, Garin drew *Helshax* and rose to face this new threat. His gaze kept traveling up, eyes widening as it did.

A shadow grew, expanding before his eyes. Five strides, ten, twenty—it stretched to loom over them, a thundercloud without bounds, prepared to spill forth storm and fury.

Around them, the white mist closed in once more. From the corner of his eye, Garin saw Wren claw her way upright, a knife clutched in her hand.

She wouldn't be enough. Neither of them would. Yet he had to try. Desperately, he searched his mind for a spell to protect them.

The ominous shadow reached its apex, forty strides tall, obscuring all light from the moon.

It began to collapse over them.

"*Jolsh rayn fend!*" Air was stolen from Garin's lungs as he recast the air dome. It buffeted back the pale mist but did nothing against the black specter.

"*Kald!*" Wren gasped, throwing up a hand against the shadow. Paltry flames leapt from her palm to scorch the writhing smoke, but if they had any effect, Garin couldn't see it.

"*Fashk!*" Light blazed from Garin's hand as he called out the cantrip. What better to counteract darkness than light? He poured what energy and will he had after the wind barrier into it.

Yet their enemy only swallowed the light, as little harmed by it as by the fire.

Out of ideas, Garin released the cantrip and held *Helshax* aloft. The sword felt puny and impotent in his hand, yet it was all he had. The black blade almost disappeared against the darkness behind it, but the gold of the runes had never shown so brightly.

The storm cloud was nearly upon them. It rushed toward them, churning the air with all the force of an avalanche and battering his eardrums.

Do you remember, Jenduit?

Even facing death, the voice resounding in his head froze Garin. He hadn't heard it in the seven years since its owner had descended with Tal into the very heart of sorcery, bearing down the false gods fighting against them. He had believed him dead.

"Ilvuan," he breathed. "Alärthoras."

No time, Listener, his dragon rumbled in his mind. *Do you remember?*

Remember?

Once, we flew together. Should we not soar once more?

Memories flooded him of that last battle, of the staggering power and freedom that filled him. Even with the shadow descending, a smile curled his lips.

Lead, he told Ilvuan, *and I will follow.*

At once, something rose from deep within him. Heat flooded through Garin, warming at first, then growing painfully hot. The surrounding area brightened. Staring at the arm with which he held up *Helshax*, he saw that his skin glowed, silver light spilling from his flesh.

The shadow reached them. Wren screamed in defiance as she fell. Garin buckled beneath the force of its power.

Then he rose, freed of his body's fetters, and Ilvuan rose with him.

Their wings spread, silver and shining, then beat once to bear them into the air. Their maw yawned, biting and tearing into the darkness all around. Claws extended forth to rip and rend.

These were weapons that could harm their foe. The darkness shrieked like a winter gale as he and Ilvuan tore through it. Its power slapped against their silver scales, but each blow was like a child's against plate armor, futile and barely felt.

Garin opened their maw to laugh and belched forth golden flames.

The fire spread as if the storm cloud was made of oil. In moments, the towering shadow was wreathed in flames, an inferno that quickly consumed it. Screams of pain and terror echoed throughout the gloomy realm, but they went unheard.

Ilvuan roared, drowning out their adversary, as it fell into ashen scraps.

In moments, the fight was over. The great shadow had burned away. The pale mist, fled at the dragon's coming, was nowhere to be seen.

Victory. Ilvuan's satisfaction radiated through every pore of Garin's being. *No realm is beyond the* ava'duala, *as all* kael'dros *shall remember.*

For several moments, Garin soared with Ilvuan overhead, marveling at the touch of moonlight on their wings, delightfully cool. Part of him wished to stay this way forever.

But Wren waited below. As did the battle beyond the rift, if it still continued.

Can you not stay? he thought to Ilvuan. The mere thought cleaved him in two. *Must you leave again?*

His dragon rumbled in that laugh of his. *A Singer never truly leaves his Listener,* Jenduit. *I will remain with you even if you cannot sense me.*

A hundred questions brewed in him, but already, their silver form plummeted back toward the ground. Garin felt an uncomfortable moment of transition, then he sank to his knees as he returned to his frail human body. He was drained to the core, yet still, he scrabbled after his soul-companion.

Ilvuan rumbled once more—then he was gone.

"Garin?" Wren shook his shoulder. "What in all the red hells just happened?"

He shook his head and clambered to his feet, barely keeping *Helshax* in hand. "No time. We have to check on the others."

"I won't object to leaving. But be ready."

He nodded, then led the way through the rift.

The gloomy realm seemed to cling to them—then they spilled forth into light. Garin blinked, blinded for a moment, then held up his sword as he scanned for enemies. Everywhere he looked, the only ones remaining were allies. His chest tightened as he saw Ashelia and Rolan crouched over a little body before the stage, then loosened as Kaleras roused. He couldn't fathom why the boy was present.

"You're late," Aelyn called over the carnage, voice weary but no less full of acid. "Just where were you two gallivanting off to?"

"Oh, stuff it," Wren muttered as she plunked down on the edge of the stage, heedless of the ichor and blood filming it.

Garin was half-inclined to join her. With the battle at an end, all the weariness of the invasion caught up with him. But, conscious of the rift yawning behind, he staggered off the stage to face it. The haunting silence issuing from it had lessened, yet it hadn't entirely disappeared.

Victory, his dragon had proclaimed. Yet he had the distinct feeling that Elendol and its people would feel the reverberations of this battle for years to come.

15
DAWN

"So," Aelyn surmised, "it appears you slew the dreadknight in its more… *primordial* form."

Garin nodded, chewing on a spiced dumpling. "So it would seem."

Red light peeked through the windows of Ashelia's bedchamber. The werelights outside altered to signal dawn's approach. They had yet to rest that night, their soon-to-be-coronated queen calling her closest advisors to council. It promised to be a long morning still, so food and drink had been provided.

They had won the battle and reclaimed all of Elendol, but Garin's hunch that it was the beginning of another struggle was already proving true. Ashelia had left two of their freshest mages to fabricate barriers around the rift, which remained open in the Lathniel banquet hall. If another dreadknight appeared, they would struggle to keep it at bay, but Aelyn was confident that within a few days, they could erect defenses even that mighty enemy could not penetrate.

Murmurs started up around their circle at Garin's answer. Aelyn snorted a laugh. "Our mighty Ivasaer and his revenant dragon," he sneered. "How we'd be lost without you."

"In this case," Wren retorted, "you would be."

Garin smiled and took another bite of his meal. He hadn't known at the time that the great shadow was the dreadknight, but it became as clear a conclusion as they could draw when they worked through the timing of the battle and the potency of their adversary. He wondered if more of them existed in that fell realm. If he could survive an encounter with another.

"It's all thanks to Ilvuan," he admitted. "The dreadknight would have overcome me and Wren otherwise."

"Your dragon survived." Though Ashelia held herself erect, her shadowed eyes and unkempt appearance betrayed her fatigue. The white crown, cloven in two during the battle, rested in her lap. "I thought he descended with Tal."

"So did I."

The silence that fell was pregnant with assumptions. Garin winced and looked away. He knew what she hoped. For if Ilvuan had survived, why would Tal not have as well?

He's gone, he thought, willing himself to believe it. *He would have already returned if he could have*.

The others seemed to think the same thing, but not even Aelyn had the callousness to speak it aloud. Yet with the gold in his eyes spinning, the elven mage couldn't be kept quiet for long.

"It would seem," Aelyn said, "that some sliver of the dragon remains embedded in you. A part potent enough to be brought out by the threat you faced—or, more likely, by entering the Voidic Realm."

"Is that what you call that place?" Wren piped up around a mouthful of food. "Not exactly subtle."

The mage flashed a tight-lipped smile. "Nor should it be, as your experiences there should have informed you. We still know little of the planes of existence beyond ours, but one thing is clear about the Void: it is the birthplace of monsters, the *kael'dros* against which the dragons once defended. And will once more," he added, "should they return to the duty they claimed to have once held tantamount."

Garin wouldn't admit it aloud, but he agreed. Aelyn's conclusions echoed Ilvuan's words and all they'd witnessed of dragons. Not all nightkin were *kael'dros*. Creatures like gryphons and cockatrices might have come from the Whispering Gods' experiments, but they behaved more or less like animals. Ghouls and the others from the Voidic Realm, though... they were true fiends, devoid of all else but a desire to harm and kill. His visit to their home only reinforced that belief.

After several moments of silence, Prime Elidyr shifted, wincing as he jostled his injuries. "Perhaps we should discuss what is to be done. Beginning with the rift?" The Prime Warder raised an eyebrow in Aelyn's direction.

Ever glad to be afforded authority, the mage straightened, the fiery light in his eyes brightening. "As soon as we are finished here, I intend to study it. I have heard of these occurrences before—permanent tears between realms. Any summoning might open a temporary rift, but it takes great power—and, in this case, mortal sacrifice—to create a lasting portal."

The moment of its creation flashed through Garin's mind. Once more, he saw Maone stabbing the twisted black knife through her bond's chest, then into her own. He closed his eyes, wishing they knew the first part about the dagger. Other than that it was old and enchanted, they knew nothing of where it had come from, nor how it had come into the false queen's possession.

Yet the mystery had caught Aelyn's interest, and little could deter him when he was on the trail of a dark secret. Garin hoped it would not be long before the mage unearthed this one.

"You believe it is permanent?" Ashelia inquired.

"Perhaps." Aelyn sounded excited at the prospect rather

than frightened, as any sane man would have been. "Given that it has shown no signs of retraction in the hours following its opening, we should assume it is here to stay."

"Very well." The queen leaned on an arm of her chair, the blow too much for even her constitution. "We will guard and ward it while you find a way to close it. Involve the Masters of the Onyx Tower in this. I will inform them they are to put all their resources toward closing it. No other research shall proceed until then—including on that knife, *Belosi*."

"Understood, Your Eminence." Aelyn bowed his head. Wren rolled her eyes at Garin. He hid a smile.

Prendyn cleared his throat, his pomposity undiminished by the sleepless night and the battle. "There are other matters requiring your attention, Your Eminence. The captives taken from House Lathniel await trial, and I have reports of a few remaining rebels causing trouble in Low Elendol."

Ashelia took only moments to answer. "The trials can wait. Time in a cell will do them some good."

Garin exchanged a look with Wren. They'd both seen Yinin taken captive. He wondered if the queen had him in mind when she said as much.

"As for the rebels," she continued, "handle them as you see fit, Captain. If battle is required, take Prime Elidyr's men to accompany you."

The Prime Warder consented to the plan, as did the Ilthasi captain, mopping sweat from his forehead.

"If that is all," Ashelia said, rising, "we should get what rest we can. Though I fear it may still be some hours away for you, Captain."

"'An Ilthasi never sleeps,' or so we like to claim."

Prendyn bowed before plodding out of the room, Elidyr following. Garin caught the beginnings of a murmured conversation between them, no doubt organizing what troops were necessary to handle the remaining rebels. He didn't relish the thought of moving to another battle and was glad Ashelia hadn't asked it of him. Tomorrow, if she didn't have a different task for him, he would offer.

Just then, sleep beckoned too strongly to resist.

Garin rose with Wren, but Aelyn remained seated. The mage leaned forward, elbows to his knees, hands steepled before his face. The tendrils in his eyes turned faster.

"And what of your son, *Kolesa?*"

Ashelia stiffened and looked over at her bed. Garin followed her gaze to the small slumbering form nestled under the blankets.

Kaleras.

Though their discussion hadn't been soft, he doubted the boy had difficulty sleeping. He'd barely been conscious as his mother carried him back from the battle.

After what he'd done, who could have expected otherwise?

Rolan had told Garin of what he'd seen as they left the Lathniel kintree. Of the sorcerous threads that his little brother had touched to throw the dreadknight back through the portal. The boy had not only seen the Lattice but manipulated it.

The same as a dragon could.

It troubled him. To have a dragon's sorcery meant Kaleras Helnor Venaliel was something Aolas had never seen before. If Tal's life was any indication, to be extraordinary meant trouble would follow him wherever he went.

He looked back at Ashelia, who still seemed lost for words. She knew as he did that the circumstances of Kaleras's birth could be responsible for this manifestation. After all, the boy had already been in her belly when she went atop Ikvaldar to vie against Yuldor and his parasitic gods. Who knew what influence exposure to such potent magic might have on an unborn child?

There was a simpler explanation, one just as likely. Kaleras was the son of Tal Harrenfel, a Fount of Blood in possession of enough sorcery to challenge deities and dragons. Perhaps he had inherited his father's power to become a different brand of

Fount. One naturally born rather than forged at the behest of the Whispering Gods.

Ashelia moistened her lips. "We will watch him. Guard him. And see what becomes of it."

Aelyn rose from his chair and drifted closer. "He is powerful, Your Eminence. Perhaps more powerful than his father."

"All the more reason he must be protected."

An edge crept into the queen's voice. Aelyn grimaced, but he didn't press the matter. "I will look into it once I have time," he said. "And when he is of age, with your blessing, I would try to teach him to control it. For his own safety."

"As will I," Garin added. "As much as I'm able."

Ashelia looked at them both and nodded. "Thank you. I…" Her eyes drifted back to her son. "I fear for him."

Garin opened his mouth to speak reassurances but had none to offer.

"Hey, wait up."

Garin withdrew his foot from the stair and turned to see Wren jogging across the platform toward him. She nodded at the nearby railing.

"Watch the sunrise with me?"

He quirked an eyebrow. "You mean the werelights changing color?"

Wren grinned. "Almost as good."

Stifling a yawn, Garin nodded and followed her to lean against the railing. The werelights shifted from the cool hues of night to the warmth of dawn. Always a spectacle to behold, he was gladdened to see them spread all throughout Elendol once more.

They stood listening to the wind rustle through the distant canopy and watching the hovering orbs of light. As the silence stretched, Garin felt Wren's gaze on him, but couldn't bring himself to meet her eyes.

"Thanks again," she said. "For saving me."

He looked at her sidelong. "Someone has to."

"You don't."

Garin turned toward her. He didn't ask what she meant. He knew that cagey look in her eyes. The tenseness that spoke of the need to flee. For all her courage in battle, it wasn't the first time Wren had tried abandoning their relationship. In this, her fears commanded her.

But is she wrong?

Wren had become a different woman over the past five years. Her broken edges had sharpened into cutting ones that made her dangerous to remain around. He loved her, but that couldn't mend what loss and rage had broken. Couldn't save her from herself.

And he wasn't certain how much longer he could stand by and watch her drown.

But he was too tired to fight, so Garin smiled like he had not a care. A smile like Tal had so often shown the world.

"Maybe I don't, but I will." He nudged her with his elbow. "You can't drive me off that easily, Moonblade."

Wren didn't rise to the goad but peered intently into his eyes. Before she turned away, her brow creased in that familiar way.

"I suppose that's good," she muttered. "Come on, we should get some rest."

Swallowing a sigh, Garin followed her back to their quarters.

16
BROTHERS

Rolan yawned as he climbed up the last of the stairs to House Venaliel's highest platform.

At the far end stood his little brother. Kaleras clutched the tines of the railing as he stared out over High Elendol. What he looked at, Rolan could only guess. It was still early morning, and the werelights, spread through the open air and around the bridges and platforms, had turned golden.

In a corner closer to the kintree stood Kaleras's nursemaid, who looked as weary as Rolan felt. She didn't seem concerned that a five-spring-old stood so close to the edge, but why should she? Even if Kaleras hadn't been uncommonly mature for his age, the residents of High Elendol were trusted early to stay safe and learn the grace necessary to navigate the branches of the kintrees. He would not fall.

If only because I'll always catch him.

Rolan crossed the planks to greet him, but he drew up short. Memories of what his little brother had done filled his mind. The threads of the Lattice sliced across his vision.

He shook his head, dismissing his concerns with a smile. This was Leras, their family's little monkey. Whatever he was capable of, it didn't change who he was.

"There's no prize for waking up early, you know," he said, ruffling Kaleras's hair as he came astride him.

His younger brother startled, then craned his neck back to glare up at him. "Quit it."

"Or what? You'll magic me off this balcony?"

Kaleras looked confused for a moment, his silver tendrils spinning faster. He lowered his gaze back to the werelights. "I wouldn't do that."

"I know. I'm just teasing." Rolan hesitated, but there was no avoiding it. "Leras, do you know what happened back there?"

The boy shook his head. "*Momua* says I used sorcery. That I must not do it again because it's dangerous."

She's not wrong. Intervening in the battle may have saved their lives, but it had put Kaleras at far too much risk for Rolan to be glad he had. Still, something about the guidance troubled Rolan. Aphorisms once spoken by Falcon surfaced in his mind.

Never hide who you are, my boy. The world is dark enough without you casting more shadows.

Though that might be true, for now, Rolan had no better advice to offer. "She's right. What you did was very dangerous. And stupid. And brave."

His little brother looked up at him again, brow creased. Rolan had to laugh. Kneeling, he came eye level with Kaleras and gripped his small shoulder.

"You must be careful, *Belosi*. Your father was powerful. And it looks like you will be, too."

Other children would have failed to grasp the gravity of his words. Rolan had no doubt that as Kaleras nodded, he understood.

"I wish I could meet him," his little brother murmured.

"I wish you could have, too. He was a great man." Rolan moved his hand to grip the back of Kaleras's head. "You will be, too, when you're grown."

"I'll try."

With a squeeze and a smile, Rolan released him and stood

to turn back to the balcony. After a moment, Kaleras reached up and took his hand. He was glad for it. For now, his brother remained a boy.

They watched the morning light reach through the thick canopy to warm their home. The day was bright, but Rolan knew darkness awaited them on some future day. With all that had occurred, it was inevitable.

He could only pray that day would be long in coming.

A NEW LEGEND DAWNS

Where one journey ends, another begins.
 Witness the return to Aolas with a new cast of characters…
 …and plenty of familiar faces as well.

LEGEND OF LERAS
Coming Soon

Follow J.D.L. Rosell on Amazon or join his email newsletter at *jdlrosell.com* so you don't miss the release.

APPENDIX A

THE CHARACTERS

Garin Dunford - Once a farm boy youth from Hunt's Hollow, he's grown into a potent sorcerer as a Listener, one who hears the Worldsong and can cast powerful spells from it. Also known as Ivasaer to the Gladelysh elves.

Wren Moonblade - The rebellious daughter of Falcon Sunstring has grown into a formidable warrior hardened by the horrors of war. Formerly a member of the Dancing Feathers troupe.

Aelyn Belnuure - An irritable elf with several titles and roles: Emissary to Avendor, Peer of Gladelyl, Master of the Onyx Tower, and itinerant mage. Adopted brother of Ashelia and Helnor Venaliel.

Ashelia Venaliel - The Crownless Queen who seeks to reign over Gladelyl. Formerly a Peer of Gladelyl, the first female Warder, a healer of the Sapphire Tower, and also reputed to have once been the lover of yore to Tal Harrenfel. Sister to Aelyn Belnuure and Helnor Venaliel. Mother to Rolan Venaliel. Former wife of Yinin Lathniel.

Rolan Venaliel - Once a young and precocious elf boy, he's grown into a fine young man of eighteen with a burgeoning need to prove himself as a bard. Son of Ashelia Venaliel and Yinin Lathniel.

Kaleras Venaliel - Also known as "Leras." A young boy of five who is serious and mature beyond his age. Son of Ashelia Venaliel and Tal Harrenfel.

Yinin Lathniel - Once a minister to Queen Geminia. Former houselord of House Venaliel and husband to Ashelia Venaliel. Father to Rolan Venaliel.

Jondual Lathniel - The Prince Consort and husband of Maone Lathniel. Houselord of House Lathniel. Father to Yinin Lathniel.

Maone Lathniel - The Queen of Gladelyl by birthright, though her right to the throne is disputed by Ashelia Venaliel. Peer of Gladelyl and leader of the Sympathist faction. Wife of Jondual Lathniel. Mother of Yinin Lathniel.

Prendyn Agarae - Once the Ilthasi captain in High Elendol, now the sole Ilthasi captain under Ashelia Venaliel.

Elidyr Ymalis - The Prime Warder of Gladelyl under the Crownless Queen, Ashelia Venaliel. First encountered during the final battles against the monster hordes of Yuldor.

HISTORICAL

Tal Harrenfel - A recent folk hero. Attributed to him are many deeds both miraculous and horrific. He met his end while bringing down the false deities of Yuldor Soldarin and the Whispering Gods. Also known as Brannen Cairn and Aristhol, among other names.

APPENDIX A

- **Kaleras Trethon** - Also known as the Impervious and the Warlock of Canturith, he is a former Magister of Jalduaen's Circle and the only warlock outside of the organization. Father to Tal Harrenfel. The man after whom Kaleras Venaliel was named.
- **Falcon Sunstring** - The half-human, half-elf Court Bard to the King of Avendor and leader of the Dancing Feathers troupe. Father to Wren Moonblade.
- **Geminia Elendola the Third** - Once the wise and calculating Queen of Gladelyl. Also known as the Gem of Elendol and the Elf Queen.
- **Helnor Venaliel** - Once the jovial Prime Warder of Gladelyl. Brother to Aelyn Belnuure and Ashelia Venaliel.
- **Yuldor Soldarin** - Once the immortal elven sorcerer who reigned as a god from atop the mountain Ikvaldar.
- **Rothaen, Haimei, and Sachiel** - Also known as the Three or the Whispering Gods. A trio of Origin sorcerers who were recorded as living during the time of the Severing and who, using the power conferred by an unbridled stream of sorcery, ascended to approximate godhood. Brought down by Tal Harrenfel and his companions.
- **Ilvuan, or Alärthoras** - Garin's dragon, who perished bringing about the downfall of Yuldor and the Whispering Gods.

APPENDIX B

THE WORLD

Continent historically known as "Aolas."

THE WESTREACH
The western countries of Aolas. Considered by its inhabitants to be the "civilized" lands.

AVENDOR
The largest and most powerful nations of the Westreach. Its populace is mostly human, but it is populated by the various Bloodlines of the western lands.

Halenhol - Capital of Avendor. Home to the Coral Castle, from which King Aldric reigns.
Hunt's Hollow - A small, unremarkable town in the East Marsh.
Jakad - An annexed territory of Avendor. Renowned for their vineyards.
Dareaux - Former capital of Jakad. A major city in Avendor.
Ruins of Erlodan - A derelict castle ravaged by time, once belonging to the warlock Erlodan.
Canturith - An ancient fortress along the Fringes

GLADELYL
The elven queendom on the outskirts of the Westreach. Possesses significant clout, particularly because of their mastery of sorcery.

Elendol - Capital of Gladelyl. Home to the kintrees of the elven noble houses, including the royal kintree, from which Queen Geminia reigns.
Yllsalar - An ancient mountain fortress along the Fringes.

SENDESH
The second largest nation of the Westreach. Predominantly human. Has a history of conflict with Avendor and suffers raids from the Yraldi to the north.

Burbay - Capital of Sendesh. The Sendeshi Protector reigns from here.

FELINAN

APPENDIX B

The third and least of the human nations. A place where, though the martial prowess flounders, the arts flourish. Their reputation is further bolstered by boasting the home of the warlocks of the Westreach.

Sisces - Capital of Felinan.
Avolice - The citadel at the center of the Jalduaen's Circle, the order of human warlocks.

DHUULHEIM
Also known as "the Dwarven Clans." A subterranean nation of dwarves that is often forced to contend with monsters from the Deep. Long has conflict simmered between the clans, inflamed by enemies from without.

CHYCHAXIL'ISK
Also known as "the Goblin Knolls." The Hoarseer tribe, led by their queen Mysx Gemfang, currently rules, though dynasties usually last only as long as the ruler lives.

OTHER
The Fringes - The hilly lands separating the Westreach from the East. Home to Nightkin coming down from the mountains.
The Yraldi Isles - The unforgiving islands in the northern Crimson Sea. Home to sea raiders who regularly invade their southern neighbor, Sendesh.
The Befa Spice Isles - The verdant islands in the southern Hushed Sea. Renowned for exports of exotic fruits and colorful weavings.

THE EAST
Also known by its inhabitants as the Empire of the Rising Sun. Though large swaths of the land remain untamed, beyond the mountains flourish various fiefs united under the Sun Emperor and the god Yuldor above him.

ISOCIL
The largest of the fiefs. Primarily occupied by humans, but also boasts all the other Eastern races. Set amid fertile plains. Also home to the capital of the Empire and the seat of the Sun Emperor.

Kavaugh - Capital of Isocil and the Empire. The Sun Palace of the Emperor is also here.
Bavay - A town renowned for its carpets.

APPENDIX B

ASPAR
The fief of Nightelves. Set amid tall, gigantic trees.

Naruah - Capital of Aspar. Home to the High Pellar, the primary priestess of Yuldor among the Nightelves.

LEDFOLD
The fief of minotaurs. Set amid plains and hills.

Haudden - The primary town of Ledfold.

RAJEYA
The fief of medusals and sylvans. Deserts, ocean shores, hills, and fjords all exist here.

Dreygoj - Capital of Rajeya.
Trader Springs - An oasis town amid the Laksis Wastes.

VRORESH
The fief of orkans. Set on a rocky and forbidding peninsula.

Ghamir Nodh - Capital of Vroresh.

AGN OMMUL
The fief of gnomes. Set in the heart of the Valanduali mountains.

Kyzan - Capital of Agn Ommul.

OTHER
Ikvaldar - The tallest mountain in Aolas. Despite its height, its rounded peak is largely dominated by a magically preserved jungle known as Paradise. It is also known to be home to the immortal sorcerer Yuldor Soldarin.
Vathda - The new home of the exiled Hardrog dwarven clan.

APPENDIX C

BESTIARY

NOVEL ANIMALS

Gilled deer - A deer found in the forests of Isocil in the East. Judging by the texture of their skin and the gills on their necks, they are suspected of living on both land and in water.

Peuma - One of the large black cats that act as protectors of the jungle Paradise atop Ikvaldar.

Sand drake - Called *zuthka* in common Darktongue. It is a large lizard habituated to arid landscapes. Its kind is used as beasts of burden similarly to the Sendeshi's use of camels.

Sonku monkey - A silver-haired monkey native to the Rainwoods in the East. It is believed to possess a touch of sorcery, for when it expresses emotion, its thick mane can glow golden.

Stor - A deer-like mount used by Gladelysh elves. As large as horses, but with long, lean legs and antlers atop their heads.

ORIGIN CREATURES

Dragon - Call themselves *ava'dual* (pl. *ava'duala*). Though now extinct, dragons are thought to have been the foremost predators of the World. Formidable in size and physicality, their mastery of sorcery was even more deadly. Legend has it they perished around the time of the Severing.

Leshi - A forest shapeshifter with a talent for illusion sorcery. These ancient creatures are believed to have been common in the time of the Origins, but have either retreated into hiding or been killed off as the mortal races encroach upon their woods.

HUMANOIDS

Centaur - A blend between an Origin and a horse. Like the Bloodlines, centaurs are intelligent and every bit as capable of language and thought as any mortal. They also possess a strong affinity for sorcery. Their solitary nature and need to protect a territory, usually a forest they name their "weald," is believed to be the reason they never established societies like the other mortal races.

NIGHTKIN: CREATED

Chimera - A lion blended with a cobra as its tail, an additional goat's head, and sometimes a small dragon's head.

Cockatrice - A large flying monster with resemblances to a farmyard rooster, but with large functioning wings, green and white feathering, and serpentine tails.

Gamayun - A small flying monster that resembles an oversized bat with humanoid features and snake-like hair.

Gryphon - A blend between a lion and a large eagle.

Ijiraq - A monster with the torso of a humanoid and the body and antlers of a caribou. It possesses an instinctive touch for illusion, making its appearance to be like that of an ordinary caribou when it suits it.

Memyke - A beetle-like monster as large as a wolf with a brown carapace impervious to magic.

Phoenix - An eagle-like bird with gold-and-red plumage and larger than a cockatrice. It is one of the deadliest Nightkin due to its faefire explosion, which can level a small city. Even after this expulsion of sorcery, the phoenix will resurrect thereafter. It has not been observed how long it takes for a phoenix to resurrect. There are no known ways to permanently kill a phoenix.

Quetzal - A flying serpent with colorful feathery wings. Often travel in a flock and take down their prey by overwhelming numbers.

Syren - A mysterious monster found among misty vales and foggy seas. Partly because of its habitat and predatory nature, no one has seen a syren and survived. Syrens appear to live together in groups. Rumored to lure travelers and sailors to their deaths by mimicking the voices of loved ones in pain or in seduction. They are believed to consume their victims down to the bones.

NIGHTKIN: SUMMONED

Soulshade - A phantom creature formed of shadows. It is summoned by the sorcerer corrupting a piece of their own soul. The summoner can command it to carry out simple tasks, as a soulshade lacks intelligence of its own.

Draugar - Similar to a zombie. It is reanimated by the inhabitance of a summoned spirit in a cadaver. This spirit takes on the characteristics of its vessel when it was alive; hence, a draugar fights and dies similar to the mortal it once was.

Ghoul - A creature summoned by Nightglyphs. Its appearance is humanoid, but with pale rotting flesh, inhuman speed, and sharp teeth and nails.

Heyl - Also called "Yuldor's Fury." Heyl is a fire devil summoned through life sacrifice and is one of the deadliest creatures to walk the World. As tall as a tower, it has two tails, four legs, and eight arms. Anything it touches burns.

Nekrot - A summoned creature that can summon others through Nightglyphs. Bearing staffs to aid in their sorcery and wearing the armor of their victims, they are most dangerous because of their ability to command armies of ghouls and witikos. They are humanoid in appearance and about as short as a dwarf.

Witiko - A creature summoned by Nightglyphs. Giants that are as skeletal as ghouls, but with a thick brown coat over their bones and a head somewhere between a wolf and a moose.

Dreadknight - A creature from the Voidic Realm. Resembles a blend between a mortal man and a black beetle. Stands taller than the mortal bloodlines and is clad in chitinous armor. A mimic of sorcery, it is dangerous to cast spells against it. Often wields a sword shaped like the horn atop its head.

CREATURES FROM THE DEEP

Brigkakor - A mountain troll that once conquered the fortress Canturith, which the warlock Kaleras later drove out.

Khaovex'das - Also called "The Darkness From the Water." A fell creature from the Deep under Dhuulheim. It is said to have killed a hundred dwarves in their copper mines before the warlock Kaleras vanquished it.

APPENDIX D

GLOSSARY

Many of the terms not referenced in the previous appendices can be found here.

- **Bloodlines** - The various races of the Westreach. Said to be created by the Whispering Gods from an ancestral race, the Origins, during an event called the Severing.
- **Canker** - Also known as *karkados*. A magical malady of mysterious origins, but it appears to be caused in part by an overindulgence in sorcery.
- **The Chromatic Towers** - The six schools of magic founded in Elendol by the Gladelysh elves.
- **Conveyance** - A sorcerous method of transferring messages to other sorcerers through paired artifacts.
- **The Creed** - The predominant religion in the Westreach, dedicated to the worship of the Whispering Gods.
- **The Cult of Yuldor** - The pejorative name given to the predominant religion of the East, dedicated to the worship of the ascended elven sorcerer Yuldor Soldarin.
- **Dancing Master** - A master of elven swordplay. Often teaches the art to pupils.
- **The Darktongue** - Though conflated in the Westreach, the Darktongue comes in two separate strands. First, there is "common" Darktongue, also called Imperial, which is the primary language of the East. Second, there is the Worldtongue variant Darktongue, which can be used for sorcery.
- **The Deep** - The bowels of the World, from which terrifying monsters originate. Most typically, the Deep refers to the area under Dhuulheim, the realm of dwarves.
- **The *Doash*** - Also known as "the World's Womb." Believed to be the source of all sorcery at the center of the World.
- **The Eternal Animus** - The latent conflict which sometimes flares into war between the Westreach and the East.
- **The Extinguished** - Also called "Soulstealers" and "the Nameless." The four servants of Yuldor Soldarin. Through their master's power, they have attained immortality, and though they can be killed, they are known to resurrect ten years later. Experts in illusion magic, the Extinguished have successfully manipulated politics across Aolas, both in the East and Westreach, to serve their master's needs.
- **Fount of Blood** - One believed to possess the blood of the World in their veins. Sorcery comes naturally to these individuals, even if they are of a Bloodline or race that is not inherently sorcerous.

APPENDIX D

Fount of Song - One believed to hear the Worldsong. Sorcery is made possible to these individuals, even if they are of a Bloodline or race that is not inherently sorcerous. Also sometimes called "Listeners."

The Four Roots - The four principles required for sorcery, according to Gladelysh elves. The First Root is an affinity for magic. The Second Root is a spoken word of the Worldtongue. The Third Root is the transfer of energy or energy potential. The Fourth Root is proper concentration paired with imagination.

Gildoil - Also known as "pissleaf." A pain reliever; an analgesic.

Gladelysh - The elvish people of Gladelyl.

Gladelyshi - The language spoken by the elves of Gladelyl.

Glyphs - Also called "runes." Written versions of the Worldtongue, they can spawn magical effects of their own when imbued with sorcery. Unpowered glyphs are used to teach magic to pupils.

Glyph-seal - A small object that carries the sigil of a Highkin House of Gladelyl. Denotes the bearer to have the authority of the House in minor matters, such as accessing reasonable resources or gaining admittance to exclusive locations.

The Greatdark - The afterlife concept of hell to those following the Creed of the Whispering Gods.

Half-kin - The term used by the Gladelyshi to refer to a mixed-blood elf, or an individual with only one elven parent. *Kolfash* is the derogatory term that means the same.

Highkin - The upper-class elves of Gladelyl. They live in High Elendol, which is built into the upper boughs of the kintrees of the city.

Heaven's Knoll - The afterlife concept of heaven for those who follow the Creed of the Whispering Gods. Also called "the Quiet Havens."

Helshax - The Darktongue word for "Lament." A bastard sword with the ability to absorb sorcery. Rumored to originate from the time of the Origins.

Heyl's Fall - The kintree that the fire demon Heyl burned down, which remains as a monument to the event.

Highkin House - A noble family of Gladelysh elves.

Ikvaldar - The tallest mountain in Aolas. Dominant across the landscape, it is known as the fortress of Yuldor Soldarin. Atop it also grows Paradise, a verdant jungle that is claimed to be Yuldor's dream that he wishes to spread to the entire World.

The Ilthasi - The secretive agents of the Queen of Gladelyl. Responsible for covertly enforcing her will, especially in the capital city of Elendol.

The Ingress of Elendol - The event during which Easterners were admitted into Gladelyl.

Jalduaen's Circle - Also known as "the Warlocks' Circle." The order of warlocks who derive their power from the mysterious god of knowledge, Jalduaen. Based in Avolice, a citadel in Felinan.

APPENDIX D

Kael'dros - Translates to "monsters" from dragon speech. The dragon term for Nightkin.

Kintree - One of the gigantic trees resembling mangrove trees that dominate Gladelyl and Elendol. The Highkin noble families make their homes within the kintrees, and their boughs form the upper part of the tree city known as High Elendol.

Lowkin - The lower-class elves of Gladelyl. In Elendol, these elves live in Low Elendol, also called "the Mire."

Medusals - The lizard-people of the East. Standing as tall as humans, they have colorful, feathery manes. They primarily live in the arid and coastal environments of the fief Rajeya.

The moons - The moons have many names. Among the names for the blue moon is "The Sorrowful Lady." Foremost among the yellow moon's names is "Cresselia."

Nightelves - The elves of the East. They live in the forest of Aspar, which is dominated by towering trees, and differ from Gladelysh elves by having cooler skin tones. Like their Westreach counterparts, Nightelves have an innate ability to use sorcery.

Nightkin - The monsters believed to be under the control of Yuldor, the immortal sorcerer who is the enemy of the Westreach. Most are said to be created by Yuldor as well.

The Nightsong - The noises that Garin hears after being possessed by what he believes to be a devil. Often accompanied by the use of sorcery.

The Obelisks - The Eastern equivalent of the Chromatic Towers of Elendol. Schools of sorcery scattered across the Empire of the Rising Sun, where mages are taught and delve into magical matters.

The Order of Ataraxis - One of the monastic orders of the Creed of the Whispering Gods.

Orkans - The hog-people of the East. Typically have skin in hues of gray and sport tusks jutting from their lips as well as other hog-like features. They primarily live in the fief Vroresh. Like humans, orkans do not have the innate ability to use sorcery, but can access it when acting as the conduit of a god. Whereas in the Westreach this takes the form of warlocks, among orkans, these magic-users are known as shamans.

The Origins - The ancestral race before the Severing of the Bloodlines. Believed to be departed from the World, they are thought to have shared features with all the races of the Westreach and the East.

Origintongue - The language of the Origins. Conflated to mean both a common speech and a sorcerous speech, though the two were likely separate.

Peer - The foremost nobility who leads an elven Highkin House.

Pellar - A priestly healer of the Nightelves.

Pyramidion - A leader of one of the Empire's Obelisks.

APPENDIX D

Quiet Havens - *See "Heaven's Knoll."*

Qorl - An elven game involving strategy to dominate one's opponent.

Ravagers - Officially called "Venators" in the East. The brutal headhunters who are said to directly serve Yuldor. Known to occasionally raid the Reach Realms.

Reachtongue - The common language of the Westreach. Assumed to have derived from a human language out of Avendor, as they have no other native tongue.

Ring of Thalkuun - A powerful artifact that makes its wearer immune to sorcery cast against them. Written on it are the words *Thalkuun Haeldar*, which translates to "The One Impervious to the Heart."

Runes - *See "glyphs."*

The Severing - The event during which it is said the Whispering Gods created the various Bloodlines in order to preserve mortalkind from the Night, who sought to destroy them.

Singer - A term by which dragons refer to themselves on account of how they perceive their use of their magic.

The *Sha'aval* - The hatching place of dragons.

Stonetongue - The common language of the dwarves of Dhuulheim.

Sylvans - The plant-people of the East. Shorter and slighter than humans, they often have appearances matching several geographies. Some have hair like wheat, others like vines, and still others resemble the coral found along the Eastern ocean shores. They have an innate sense of sorcery, though it appears to be limited.

The Worldheart - Said to be a stone of sorcery possessed by Yuldor Soldarin, which grants him access to great power and makes him the Master of Time and Material.

The Worldsong - The magical song that emanates from the World's core, only heard by dragons and those termed "Listeners."

The Worldtongue - The sorcerous language used by magic-users of the Westreach. Combined with the other principles of the Four Roots, speaking a word or combination of words of the Worldtongue will produce a spell.

Velori - The bastard sword wielded by Tal Harrenfel. Said to be forged and enchanted by goblin smiths from ages past. Its blade is etched with glyphs that glow a gentle blue. The full extent of its sorcery is not known, but it appears to keep its sharp edge and resist rust.

Yinshi - A dried red herb with a peppery scent. Often used as an aid for concentration by mages, as ingesting it produces an obsessive state of mind.

Yethkeld - Means "hellfire" in Gladelysh. A yellow combustive powder used as a catalyst for minor spells.

ACKNOWLEDGMENTS

A huge round of thanks to:

Kaitlyn, my wife and first reader, who knocked me down a peg once more (in the best possible way);

Sarah Chorn for her thoughtful editing and being willing to dive into Aolas blind;

Shawn Sharrah for his keen proofreading and perpetual enthusiasm;

René Aigner for creating yet another fantastic cover illustration;

And thank you, *dear reader*, for returning to Elendol with me. I hope you enjoyed revisiting the cast from Legend of Tal as much as I did.

~ Josiah
J.D.L. Rosell

BOOKS BY J.D.L. ROSELL

Sign up for future releases at jdlrosell.com.

LEGEND OF TAL
1. A King's Bargain
2. A Queen's Command
3. An Emperor's Gamble
4. A God's Plea
A Battle Between Blood (*Novella*)

RANGER OF THE TITAN WILDS
1. The Last Ranger
2. The First Ancestor
3. The Hidden Guardian
4. The Wilds Exile

THE RUNEWAR SAGA
1. The Throne of Ice & Ash
2. The Crown of Fire & Fury
3. The Stone of Iron & Omen

THE FAMINE CYCLE

1. Whispers of Ruin
2. Echoes of Chaos
3. Requiem of Silence

Secret Seller *(Prequel)*

The Phantom Heist *(Novella)*

GODSLAYER RISING

1. Catalyst
2. Champion
3. Heretic

ABOUT THE AUTHOR

J.D.L. Rosell was swept away on a journey when he stepped foot outside his door and into *The Hobbit*. He hasn't stopped wandering since.

In his writing, he tries to recapture the wonder, adventure, and poignancy that captivated him as a child. His explorations have taken him to worlds set in over a dozen novels and five series, which include Ranger of the Titan Wilds, Legend of Tal, The Runewar Saga, and The Famine Cycle.

When he's not off on a quest, Rosell enjoys his newfound hobby of archery and older pastimes of hiking and landscape photography. But every hobbit returns home, and if you step softly and mind the potatoes, you may glimpse him curled up with his wife and two cats, Zelda and Abenthy, reading a good book or replaying his favorite video games.

Follow along with his occasional author updates and serializations at jdlrosell.com or contact him at josiah@jdlrosell.com.

Printed in Great Britain
by Amazon